Set Me Free

Ann
Clare
LeZotte

SCHOLASTIC PRESS / NEW YORK

Text copyright © 2021 by Ann Clare LeZotte
Jacket illustration copyright © 2021 by Julie Morstad
All rights reserved. Published by Scholastic Press, an imprint
of Scholastic Inc., *Publishers since 1920*. SCHOLASTIC,
SCHOLASTIC PRESS, and associated logos are trademarks and/or
registered trademarks of Scholastic Inc.

The publisher does not have any control over and does not
assume any responsibility for author or third-party websites or
their content.

No part of this publication may be reproduced, stored in a
retrieval system, or transmitted in any form or by any means,
electronic, mechanical, photocopying, recording, or
otherwise, without written permission of the publisher. For
information regarding permission, write to Scholastic Inc.,
Attention: Permissions Department, 557 Broadway, New
York, NY 10012.

While inspired by real events and historical characters, this is
a work of fiction and does not claim to be historically accurate
or portray factual events or relationships. Please keep in mind
that references to actual persons, living or dead, business
establishments, events, or locales may not be factually
accurate, but rather fictionalized by the author.

Library of Congress Cataloging-in-Publication Data available

ISBN 978-1-338-74249-7
1 2021
Printed in the U.S.A.   23
First edition, September 2021
Book design by Marijka Kostiw

R0460839683

FOR

ALL THE DEAF

AND HARD OF HEARING KIDS

AND TEENS AFFECTED

BY COVID-19

"She is like a little safe, locked,

that no one can open. Perhaps

there is a treasure inside."

—WILLIAM GIBSON,
The Miracle Worker

Part
One

Chapter One

I still get land sickness. Watching the heavy sea swell till I fear it will spill over, I take deep breaths to combat my nausea. I sympathize with small creatures caught in its great pull. What if they crash on the rocks?

Amid the beach's white, tan, amethyst, and black grains of sand is a sailors' dumping ground. I spy lobster traps, broken ships' masts, and a cracked cutlass that once hoisted anchors. It's like a tackle graveyard. A wheelbarrow is stained from carrying thousands of gutted fish. Small iridescent flies gather on it. Sprouts of bright green grass surround the blanket where I sit.

I picked this unlikely spot, behind Ezra Brewer's house, to write. I'm penning a history of the deaf population on our island, which is uncommonly large. One in four born in Chilmark in the west of Martha's Vineyard, off the coast of Massachusetts. I've come to know every inch of the land I daily explore and record, so anything new is welcome. But lately, my flow of ideas and words has slowed to a trickle. And because I think in a combination of signs, pictures, and a stream of feeling that resembles music, it takes some time to get it on paper.

I'm fourteen now. One would think that I have more free time, as my schooling finished when I was twelve, but there are more chores to do, more expectations to keep the household as I grow, so I may one day run my own. Is that my sole ambition?

I spot a fishing pole I've never seen. It's stuck in the silt, leaning at an angle. Lightning must have hit it; it's galvanized black. I wish my imagination could frame it as a mystical object—a medieval sword caught in granite waiting to be released by its rightful owner— but my interest dribbles away.

I envy my best friend Nancy's pursuits. She lives near Boston with her uncle, Jeremiah Skiffe, and is learning to be a concert pianist. She is a passionate and dedicated student, but also has many pastimes. She's joined a group called the bluestockings, who advocate for the rights of women. I find the ideas of self-reliance that Nancy has shared intriguing. Why can I no more own property than vote?

A gust of wind tickles my hands and neck. The way the breeze moves about me is almost a sound. I don't need to hear it whistling to know it's passing through.

I miss the adventures Nancy and I used to have together. I've seen her only once since she left the Vineyard. We exchange letters as frequently as we can. If I find a local fisherman leaving for the city, it takes only a week for the post to arrive. Otherwise, lonely months pass without news.

When I think of her uncle, I can't help but feel a sting. He was involved in the accident that killed my brother, George, and fled before the inquest. It was a cowardly maneuver. Still, I am grateful to him for helping Nancy flee her abusive parents. I hope to visit her someday.

But the thought of Boston makes me break out in a chill. I dream of it sometimes, being held captive in a foreign city, never knowing if I'd return home. Sometimes, when I wake, I cannot move my hands and fear I can no longer speak, just as I felt then.

The pen I'm holding drips ink on my skirt. I blot the stain with a piece of rag paper. This is useless! I promised Papa I'd be back at the farm by midday. I squint toward the sun high in the sky, pack up my writing materials, and walk toward home.

As I come around Ezra Brewer's house, my old friend sits in his favorite wicker chair. His body is lean with muscle, but he's asthmatic and walks with a slight limp. He uses an economy of signs, adapting words to his bent hands.

He must note my concern because he signs, "The ague left me weakened but didn't rob me of my spite, gal."

A shivering fever swept the island last year. Thank the Lord, our family was spared. The Wampanoag people were the hardest hit. People in all four of their communities suffered—Aquinnah, Chappaquiddick, Takemmy, and Nunnepog. There were about four thousand in number at First Contact; today there are not even one thousand.

"From what ship is that broken cutlass?" I ask, hoping for a stirring tale.

"Nay, I can't remember," he says. His fingers shine silver from scraping scales off fish with his trusty knife. There's a bucket at his feet. His one-eyed cat, Smithy, mother to my Yellow Leg, tries to scoop her share of cod. When he lifts her into his lap, I see her whiskers have grayed to match her master's.

"Just as well. I'm needed at the barn," I tell him.

A mischievous smile spreads across his face. "Can't say I envy you, Mary. But I suppose the time is for the young. Even the Irish."

He refers to our farmhand Eamon's nephews, recently arrived from Ireland.

"I'm tired of your bigoted notions," I sign.

"Me?" He points to himself. "Why should I mind anyone who doesn't harm me?"

He reaches for a pipe in his pocket and a bottle by his chair. Finding neither, he scowls.

"What do I need good health for?" he signs. "Yes, the time is for the young. You'd better get going." Ezra Brewer seems timeless to me, neither young nor old, like the sea. Why is he suddenly contemplating age? I leave him to it and start for home.

I used to make up stories as I walked. Fancies of my imagination. That dried up soon after I was rescued and returned to the island. Now I make lists of chores and check them off in my mind. There's safety in routine.

When I reach the high road, I empty sand from my shoes and tread a familiar path. I stoop to pick up a piece of petrified driftwood. The sides are strangely smooth, and the top is crystallized. It took millions of years to make this. I feel a spark of inspiration, but I doubt I'll get any work done where I'm going.

Chapter Two

Papa is out in the fields with Eamon. His three nephews sleep with him on pallets in the barn. I promised I'd keep an eye on them for an hour. It's like wrangling ginger foxes. When I arrive, they are set to sweeping the floor. More like kicking up dust. With their uncle out of sight, they chase a lamb in circles till I stand in their way and they nearly knock me down.

I clear the butchering table in the barn to lay out my writing supplies. Dipping pen in ink, I write:

History is for beggars. We are hungry for scraps from the table of Time. We want to know who, what, where, when, how, and, most of all, why. Take this sample of petrified driftwood. Was it created here, on this idyllic island, or did it wash in with the tide?

I feel stomping through the floor. Little Liam appears and gestures for me to follow him. He wears a sly smile and kicks hay on the floor. He has a mop of red curls and skin as pale as milk but scattered with freckles. He sticks his tongue through a large gap between his two front teeth to make himself look even more suspect.

"What now?" I sign irritably. Just yesterday they set fire to a bale of hay while climbing up with a candle in hand. He doesn't understand me.

Liam is jumping up and down. I'm sure the other two boys are giggling up a storm in the adjacent room, where we dip the sheep to rid them of parasites. I'm nervous to see what they've gotten up to while my attention was diverted.

I place the wood on my papers and rise from the barrel where I'm sitting. Liam slips around the corner, then peeks to see if I'm coming. The new skirt I made is more restricting than my old clothes, but I pick up my pace nonetheless.

"On my way," I sign to no one in particular.

My reaction must be all they hoped for. I stand, mouth agape, staring at the shivering creature. Christy and Finn, twins with their matching straw-like nutmeg hair and wide brown eyes, are standing nearby, their hands and feet dyed as red as the lamb's wool. I rush to look in the bath and it's full of crushed cranberries and buckets of water. The boys are rolling on the floor, clutching their bellies, in near hysteria. I shake my head and look for a clean rag. Try as I might, I can't wipe the color from the baby's tufty coat. Someone will have a red shirt for Christmas, from wool dyed before it was shorn.

When I lead the lamb out of the barn and back to the flock, his mother barely recognizes him. And I have to laugh a little too.

The wind kicks up. As I turn from the paddock to the barn, my papers come flying at me like a flock of inky birds. They scatter and I try to gather them, but the sheep munch them along with the grass. Alas, I just wrote my first clear observation in months and now the critics will turn it to mulch.

I return to the barn to clean the tub, though not the boys who climb the ladder fast and pull it up to the loft, their white faces with dark eyes watching me. I'm ashamed to say I have a small fit. The time may be for the young, but I don't have patience for wild little boys. I imagine if three nieces had come from County Galway, they wouldn't vex me so. I suppose I'm still an object of humor as I rave with my hands, shriek, and kick a bale of hay.

Eamon must hear and comes running. He yells and signs, "Jesus, Mary, and Joseph!"

I leave the scene and grab hold of a nearby fence, counting backward from fifty till I start to calm down.

It's just my luck that my former schoolmate Sarah Hillman chooses this time to pass by in a carriage with her mother. Sarah's beau, Nathaniel Hamilton, lives up the high road. They must be visiting for tea. Perhaps Reverend Lee will join them. Sarah and Nate make doe eyes at each other in church. As the horses halt, I try to smooth my stained gown and tuck the hair falling out of its bun.

"Mary," Sarah speaks and signs, "you seem distressed and look disheveled. May we offer some assistance?"

I can't hear tones, but I'm an expert at reading facial expressions. This one is smug.

"I'm doing quite well," I sign while meeting her gaze.

I see her huff. "Honestly, Mary, your bearing and manners aren't proper at your age."

"You're only one year and some months older than I," I remind her.

"And what a difference it makes!" she signs, her apple-green eyes flashing.

"It was pleasant to see you, Mrs. Hillman, ma'am," I lie before walking away. As I approach our house, it occurs to me: Does Mama wish we were paying a call to a proper young gentleman? Is that all she wants for my future?

I leave my dirty shoes inside our front door. My room is at the back of the house, adjacent to the kitchen. After putting away my writing implements and the piece of driftwood, I join Mama in the kitchen. I tell her what the nephews did. She smiles broadly. Observing my scowl, she signs, "Sounds like something you and Nancy would have done."

"We never did anything like that," I tell Mama.

"You never thought of it," she replies, shaking her head.

I dry the dishes and recall some of my exploits with Nancy. The time we haunted Littlewoods as specters wrapped in sheets. That led to a falling-out and reconciliation, which wasn't unusual for us. Sitting in an oak tree and throwing acorns at passersby. And when my brother, George, was alive, forming a trio and riding a riptide or clambering up the cliffs without fear for safety.

"Have I lost my sense of adventure?" I ask Mama.

She puts down a dish and signs, "I don't think so. You've matured, and there's nothing wrong with being more cautious after everything that happened."

Even now, the memory feels fresh and disturbing.

"I suppose that's true," I sign. "Still, sometimes I feel I've become too settled."

"I like feeling settled," Mama signs.

She's prodding me to be more like her. What if I don't meet her expectations? Can I live my life in one place and be content?

We finish the dishes and move on to folding laundry.

"I haven't received a letter from Nancy lately," I sign.

"Would you put the large trivet on the table?" Mama signs too quickly, averting her gaze. "I've made a big pot of stew, and Papa will be in soon." Is she keeping something from me?

As I'm setting the table, a cool wind tickles my back. Papa must have come in the kitchen door. When I feel a tapping at the back of my knee, I know he brought our herding dog, Sam.

I turn around and squat to pet him. I try to rub

his scruff, but he turns his rump to me. I scratch it vigorously with both hands. When I look up, Mama wrinkles her nose, and I lead Sam back out the door. Papa is at the sink washing his arms up to his elbows. Yellow Leg is perched on a chair near the hearth. She looks like a bread loaf with her legs tucked under her.

We fill our plates and say grace.

Papa says, "An unusual lamb joined the flock today."

I look to Mama's bright smile.

"I hope you don't expect any grandchildren," I sign.

Papa bursts into hearty laughter.

"Mary!" Mama uses my name sign, brushing the fingers of her right hand on her cheek. "That's not appropriate for table, and I wouldn't make those decisions now. You're still young."

"Which is it, Mama?" I sign while gulping a carrot. "Today you said I've matured and I'm less adventurous. While Sarah told me I don't have proper bearing or manners."

"I resent that remark about your manners," Mama signs. "We've raised you well. You're poised between childhood and womanhood, and I remember how awkward that felt."

I sigh and push my chair back from the table.

"I still lose my balance just looking out at the sea," I sign. "I loved to ride the waves before my ordeal took away a little part of me. I'm still trying to guess who I am."

"That's natural," Mama assures me, though her eyes look worried.

Papa raises his glass and signs with the other hand.

"To our Mary, in all her beautiful contradictions. May the Lord keep her and always guide her way!"

I can say amen to that.

After I help Mama clean the kitchen, I go to my room and quickly scribble the lines I wrote in the barn before I get into bed. I knead Yellow Leg's coat, while the moon, a shining, young woman's face, watches me through the window. Lying awake, I make plans for tomorrow. Am I courageous enough to follow through?

Chapter Three

I tread crisp grass and early fallen leaves as I haul water from the well into the kitchen and fill the kettle. I sweep the floor and dust the furniture, motes swirling in the early autumn apple-cider-colored sunlight. Mama works with me, probably humming a tune, with a rhythm to her movements. I never get that feeling from housework. Sometimes it comes when I'm writing. But never at times like these, tripping over the hem of my skirt as I try to usher dirt over the threshold and back into the yard. I only succeed in kicking it up again.

I haven't given up hope of becoming a schoolteacher. Miss Hammond retired when she married the blacksmith, Mr. Pye, and she became with child. She's promised to apprentice me when things settle down. In the meantime, I keep up my learning with George's books. But I can feel myself grow more restless and impatient with each day that passes.

Lost in my thoughts, I accidentally drop the char bucket, and ashes scatter. I anxiously reach for the broom, but Mama takes it from my hands, her expression gentle but strained.

She signs, "Why don't you have one of your walks? It invigorates your body and often clears your mind." It is a politic suggestion, especially since I see the color rising in her cheeks as her patience reaches its end like steam in the kettle.

I decide not to change out of my work clothes before I leave. I will explore the tidal flats while the tide is out. I need to shake myself out of this daily torpor.

I walk swiftly past the farm, crossing my fingers that I'm not spotted by the little rogues. I pick up a birch stick and tap it on the stone wall that frames the high road. I pass Mr. Pye's workshop. Hammer striking iron creates a vibration I feel in my chest. I stop to enjoy the one-note tune.

Suddenly, I'm pelted with stones. I swerve to face my assailants. They're on a covert spying mission, but they've left signs everywhere. Not least of all, a ginger head peeking up behind the wall. If I don't want company, I'll have to beat them at their own game.

18

I raise my hands like claws and charge toward them, growling. They scatter, and I continue on my way, grinning like a possum.

Estuary Lane is obscured by bunches of little bluestem grass turned a cinnamon color signifying autumn. Not many come here. Oyster farmers walk the tidal flats when they're not flooded. Nancy's cousin, Jeb Skiffe, went exploring and never came back.

I read a sign on the path. *CAUTION: Do not go out on the mud flats at low tide. The oncoming tide creates a quicksand effect and is very dangerous.*

I gulp. Even Nancy never suggested we explore here. Can I conquer what we weren't bold enough to try when we were children? Is it possible I'm now the braver one?

I wade through the grasses and walk down a hill. Reaching the shore, a line of wrack and seashells indicates the high-water mark. The tangled seaweed's pungent odor fills my nostrils. Stepping past it, I view miles of fine-grained silt under a pristine blue sky. A seabed without a sea.

I remove my shoes and stockings. I tread the muck, which is surprisingly firm. It's not smooth but sculpted

19

by the waves. I take ten steps before I trust the ground not to pull me under. I wouldn't be able to hear the tide rushing in.

I look ahead, my hand shielding my eyes from the sun. I'm free from household chores and the town's proprieties. Feeling giddy, I lift my skirt to my knees and skip and twirl. With one big toe, I scrawl my name in the mud.

Glancing back, I can't see my shoes and stockings anymore. Still, there's something about this wide expanse that makes me keep going. It's as though the horizon keeps receding and I want to catch up.

The exposed oyster reefs have a rough, bunched-up surface. I bend to look at the clusters of shells. They have the same white-gray color of wasps' nests. I will let them be.

A small rivulet unsticks the soles of my feet from the wet sand. I don't notice how long I have been out here, how the sun changes position and shadows shift or disappear. I ignore at first the water that begins to trickle around my toes, until it is almost near my ankles. Have I been paying so little attention? Just as in childhood when searching for beach glass could absorb me for lazy hours till I felt the sting of sunburn. I was so dead set on my adventure that the tide has started to come in and I paid it no heed!

I turn to see the shore is a long way off. Water gradually floods the path I trod to get here. My heart beats a little faster, and when I take a step, my foot sticks just enough to make a print in the sand; it sucks at my skin as I pull my leg back to meet the other.

Urgency bubbles up inside of me. I run and almost trip as my foot sinks in the sand, pulling me down on one knee. I pick myself up and try to tread more carefully and hurry at the same time.

I'm wet up to my thighs and try to forget the story of Jeb Skiffe. As Ezra Brewer tells it, by the time other oystermen heard his call, he was buried up to his chest in quicksand with the tide rushing in. One of the men fastened a rope around his waist and the others held on as he braved the frigid, murky water. He pulled and pulled, trying to release Jeb until he lost his strength and let go. When the tide went out, all that was left was one of Jeb's shoulders, like a rock embedded in the mud.

The sea is up to my hips, and my legs are sinking,

but I can see the shore ahead. Why did I have to scare the boys away? Why didn't they persist in following me?

I push my whole body forward with great effort, which brings on a coughing fit. Just then, I feel a rope in front of me and desperately grab on. My head goes underwater as I'm pulled. I wrap the rope around my wrists and twist and turn with the current. I can't tell if I'm getting close to land until my belly is scraping sand and I feel cool air on my back.

I lift my head and see no one. Then moccasins and the hem of a broadcloth skirt appear. The rope goes slack, and someone reaches for my hand. A firm grip raises me up until I'm looking into the brown-and-gold-flecked eyes of Sally Richards.

"Thank you," I sign.

She makes the sign for "horse" and points down the beach to her brown stallion, Bayard, once my brother George's colt. She must have tossed the rope, then jumped on his back to have the power to free me.

I'm shivering in my soaked gown and tangled wet hair. My shoes and stockings were washed away. Sally removes a blanket from Bayard and puts it across my shoulders. My gait is unsteady. We walk with arms encircling each other's backs. I've always been wary of the horse with rolling eyes who stomps and snorts, but he helped save me. Sally mounts and I climb up behind her. All my muscles ache. I lean against her upright back as she takes the reins, and the stallion trots up the beach at the surf line.

I'm relieved she doesn't question me, just as I ignore the net of oysters hanging from the saddle.

We stop at a spot I didn't know existed. When we dismount, I see a fire pit with several logs set around it as seats. I won't reveal this place to villagers. I sit and watch Sally ignite a blaze with a fire-starting kit of flint and steel. I carry nothing useful with me. Sally takes a small cast-iron kettle, a pewter cup, and a pouch containing dried herbs from her saddlebag. She collects water at a nearby spring and sets the kettle at the edge of the fire to heat. She scoops some of the herbs, wintergreen leaves mainly, into the kettle, making a warm brew for me to drink. The taste is subtle, a mellow mint, with a bitter undertone. Grandmother Harmony used to make wintergreen-leaf tea, as many colonists did

23

during the war, when black tea could not be easily obtained from England.

I begin to relax. At age thirteen, Sally is already knowledgeable about medicines and learning to become an animal doctor. In Wampanoag society, women are leaders. I wonder if Nancy's bluestockings know this.

"Thanks, again," I sign. "You arrived just in time." The thought of what could have happened seems too big and frightening to contemplate. It makes my chest tighten. What would my parents have done if they'd lost me too? Mama barely survived George's death. When I was younger, it never felt as if there were consequences, but everything is different now.

Sally smiles. "Not at all. I was down-island at the Skiffe farm and decided to take the south beach route home rather than the high road."

"How are Nancy's parents?" I ask.

Sally shakes her head. "Visits to their farm are never pleasant. Some of their flock have bluetongue."

I look at her inquiringly.

"Lesions on their hooves spread by biting insects. I told Mr. Skiffe to separate the affected sheep, shield them from the elements and give them plenty of water. A poultice of collected herbs should be applied. But he's decided it's foot rot and is ready to cull the herd!"

"They won't follow your directions?" I ask with concern.

"They told me to leave without paying me for my time," she signs.

"It makes me angry you're treated that way," I sign.

"Though I have my mother's light brown skin, my long hair doesn't fall straight. Everyone knows my father was an African slave and we're mixed with European blood. That always sets me apart from 'just an Indian' when I come to Chilmark. And sometimes in Aquinnah too."

"It's not fair you should be persecuted for your parents' marriage," I sign. "And not compensated for your services."

"The notion that an Indian should look one way vexes me! Your English townsfolk are not so open about the mixing of their heritage." She leans forward and stares ahead.

"Anyway, I gathered my fee from the beach." She winks and points to the net of oysters.

"Will your mother make a stew of them?" I ask, my empty stomach grumbling.

"Mary," she informs me, "my mother died." The news makes me startle and feel like curling up in a ball and sobbing.

For years, Helen Richards was a washerwoman in homes like the Skiffes, and a talented jewelry maker. She was frail as long as I knew her. There was a time when she was a regular presence at our farm. Less prideful but more poised than Sarah Hillman. Even knowing my mother's prejudices, Helen brought us meals when George died and Mama couldn't rise from her bed. I should have inquired when I didn't see her.

"No one told me," I sign, feeling guilty that I didn't try to keep in contact. There's much separation between my community and Sally's, and tensions often run high. Recently, a Wampanoag man in Chilmark was shot in the back for being an alleged horse thief. Our council ruled the English settler acted in self-defense.

"Losing a loved one is the hardest thing to bear," I sign. "I've lost a brother. I can't imagine losing either of my parents. Was it the ague?"

26

Sally nods, her eyes brimming with tears. "I miss her. But she's traveling to the ancestors. Papa's burying his grief in another expedition. I hope he returns soon."

Sally's father, Thomas Richards, used to be Papa's farm worker until he took up whaling.

"Who's looking after you?" I ask.

"I am living with my aunt and uncle until my father returns from whaling."

"I'm a year older than you, Sally," I sign. "And I'm not sure which direction I'm headed. You seem much more certain of your path."

Sally ignores the compliment. "What were you doing on the flats?"

"I guess I wanted a daring adventure like the old days," I confess, suddenly feeling childish.

"There are different ways to be bold as we grow," she tells me.

"Like Sarah Hillman and her beau, Nate?" I ask. "I don't have that sort of interest."

"I don't know them." Sally smiles. "But I'll bet you can find a way to be courageous without almost killing yourself."

"Hope," I sign, my fingers flapping like wings.

"Now I'm hungry," Sally signs, patting her stomach.

She grabs the net of oysters. I place them in the rinsed-out bowl and move them over the heat until the shells crack open. We gulp the plump, springy insides.

The sun is beginning to set. We mount Bayard, follow the shoreline, and ride up the back pastures of our farm. When we dismount, I thank Sally again, bringing the open palm of my hand down from my chin.

"I owe you," I tell her. "All you have to do is ask."

"That's not why I helped you."

"Nevertheless," I sign.

Chapter Four

I won't let the boys see me looking like a drowned rat. I run home, slip in the front door, and tiptoe toward the kitchen. Mama must be upstairs in her sewing room. I close my bedroom door behind me, strip to my skin, and put on a clean shift and shawl. I glance in the looking glass. I have small abrasions on my face. I loosen my blond hair and vigorously brush it to remove the sand and untangle the knots. I look reasonably intact when I step into the kitchen.

Mama is lugging in wood through the back door. It's not a chore she usually does. I go to help her.

"Oh, Mary, you're back," she signs with only one hand. It's hard to grasp her meaning.

I'm deciding how much to tell as I help her drop the logs by the hearth. But her back is turned, and I think she's speaking without signing. I can't catch her eye. What's wrong?

I grab her hands to get her attention and try to read her facial expression, but she averts her gaze.

"Mama," I sign, "please tell me what's wrong?"

She looks around, perhaps for Papa, who must still be working.

"I feared you weren't coming back," her hands whisper.

"I lost track of time . . . and stayed out too long . . . I'm fine, Mama," I stammer with signs.

"I should have told you days ago, when it arrived. I've kept it in my apron, half hoping it would disappear or I had imagined it."

"Don't understand," I sign.

The back door swings open with a bang. The familiar vibrations of Papa stomping his boots comfort me.

"You give to her?" Papa asks Mama.

"Not yet," she signs.

He nods to her, reassuringly.

"Mary," he signs, affectionately brushing his cheek. "Know you think seriously before sending a response."

"Letter?" I ask Mama. Perhaps Nancy has an opportunity for me, some way I could be brave and useful.

Mama nods, her sky-blue eyes dull. She reaches into her apron and pulls out a folded paper. Papa takes it from her hand and gives it to me. It's addressed to me, but it's been opened and read. That's not like Mama. I notice, as she must have, that it's not Nancy's handwriting. What's this missive that has put a fright in Mama? I sit in Papa's chair by the hearth and read.

Dear Mary,

I hope you'll welcome this correspondence. It must be three years since I last saw you. I pray you made it safely back to your island. My former employer, Dr. Minot of Beacon Hill, could find no word of you.

I'm recently in service at a large estate called the Vale. The family resides in summertime, but staff stays on year-round. My mistress's niece is hidden away in an upstairs room. I put her age at eight years.

I was told she is mad and cruel. She gasps loudly and makes odd clicking sounds. Because of her behavior, she's kept locked up. The local physician regularly sedates her. I've come to realize that she is deaf-mute.

I remember little of the hand language you taught me. But I wonder if it could soothe the child's misery. I told the butler I might know of a tutor. He said an animal trainer would be more useful.

You taught me not to judge by appearances and never to
give up hope. I'm enclosing the address. I've permission to offer
you the position. You'd receive room and board and a small
compensation. I pray you will join us. I must tell you, there
may be more to the matter than I suspect.

Sincerely,
Miss Nora O'Neal

I look to my parents, whose hands are flying.

"It's some sort of trap," Mama signs, pacing in front of the kitchen hearth. "They want her back."

"They wouldn't dare," Papa signs. "They did the right thing once they knew Noble had lied." Mama and I react to the name in different ways; she is fretful, and maybe a bit guilty, while I feel a spike of fear. It all comes rushing back.

Andrew Noble was a scientist who came to our island to discover why so many are born deaf. My family was grieving George's death, and Andrew curried favor with Mama, until he absconded with me and brought me to Boston as a "live specimen" in a cruel experiment. Providence, my own wits, and a network of Vineyard sailors delivered me home in the middle of a maelstrom.

Papa looks into my eyes and signs, "You are old enough to make your own decisions, and this must be your choice."

I knew Nora for most of our acquaintance as Miss Top. I can see in my mind the way she used to bob and twirl and throw her hands up as she moved, as if she were always remembering something she had to do. She was kind to me, if misguided, when I was terrified and alone. I don't think that she would try to trick or hurt me. She helped rescue me. And if she wants to do the same now for another . . .

Mama looks at me with pleading eyes.

"Must go to bed." I lay my cheek on the palm of my hand. "I'm exhausted and I don't know what to make of this." I clutch the letter in my hand.

"Won't you have dinner?" Mama seizes on a tangible fact to keep the phantoms at bay. I can't blame her for hiding the letter from me. The incoming tide throwing me back and forth over the flats was less of a shock.

"I ate earlier," I sign. "Maybe I'll take a cup of tea to bed. But I crave rest and cannot think on any of this now."

"Yes." Mama nods her dainty fist. Moments later, she places a cup of strong black tea on my night table. I sip, but it doesn't keep me awake. My last thought floats away to another world. My pillow sags with the weight of dreams. My fingers dance on the quilt pulled up to my chin, working out at night what I'll decide in daylight.

Chapter Five

I wake early and turn my attention to my soiled work clothes. Fingering the bodice of the dress, I find it's not only smeared with mud but badly torn. I've a working dress only recently outgrown. It'll fit well enough till I make another, though my old shoes will pinch my toes. Stoking the hearth fire, I feed the garments to the growing flames. I use the poker to make sure there's not a scrap left to provoke curiosity.

I wash and change into my new green gown. The bodice has a high collar and long, fitted sleeves, but it's soft as feathers. Mama says it makes my hazel eyes brighter. I twist my thick hair two or three times before I get the style right. I wear the necklace Helen Richards made for me. It matches the dress. She put great care into her art. The only advice I've heeded from Sarah is to put your best assets together. I'm going visiting today. I leave a note for Mama on the kitchen table.

Outside, I'm surprised to find the remnants of a

storm. Tree branches are scattered in the yard. The earth must be soaked to its core. Worms have come out of their flooded holes. Redbirds swoop to eat them and busily rebuild their nests. There's a freshness in the air.

I'm latching our front gate when Mr. Butler slows down his oxcart.

"I slept without interruption," I sign. "You?"

It's a joke between deaf townsfolk that we are not disturbed by loud noises that keep others awake. But Mr. Butler looks tired rather than amused.

He creates a vivid scene with signs. "Sky lightning—*flash*—strikes barn, burns."

"Livestock, escape?" I sign.

The look of relief on his face reassures me. We say "good day" with a nod of our heads. I couldn't share this fluency in sign language anywhere else but on my island. Before my ordeal, I took it for granted.

I walk past the vicarage. Reverend Lee is nowhere in sight. I follow a wrought-iron fence. It's been too long since I've visited George's grave. In a few years, I'll be older than he. Lines from a poem come to mind: *Gather ye rose-buds while ye may / Old Time is still a-flying.* I wipe the dirt from the stone and sign, "My

36

brother, how would you advise me?" I imagine his pragmatic reply: "The scientific method. Be sensible, think it through. Seek counsel from an expert in the field."

I follow that advice and tread down the high road to the Pye farm. I inhale the sea air, which I prefer to summer roses. Geese fly over in a V formation. The house adjoining Mr. Pye's shop looks tidier, more welcoming than when he lived alone. The porch is repainted, and there's a wreath on the door. I knock, regretting I didn't bring a gift of cake or lavender soap.

Mrs. Pye is rounder and her cheeks glow. In March, she gave birth to baby Lissy, whom she holds on her hip as she welcomes me into her home. She sets her down and signs, "What brings you here?"

I hand her Miss O'Neal's letter. While she reads, I pull Lissy onto my lap and bounce her lightly until I feel her laugh. I would make a good older sister to an agreeable child.

Mrs. Pye prompts me. "My goodness, that's quite a story. But what have you come to ask me, Mary?"

I frown thoughtfully, trying to find the right words.

"I guess I want to know if someone who's never learned any language can be taught," I sign.

She laughs and shakes her head helplessly. "Of all my students, you always asked the most challenging questions."

I smile, dipping my head.

"The simple answer is, I don't know," she signs. "Common sense would have me tell you no. As babies, we have no language." She gestures to Lissy, who is babbling with finger signs. "We learn by listening or watching others as we begin to understand the world around us. For someone who is older . . ." She shrugs.

"Maybe the sounds she makes are a private language," I suggest. It's a strange thought, that another deaf girl might have a completely different way of understanding everything I take for granted.

Mrs. Pye must see something cross my face because her expression is gentle and sympathetic. "I must think on it," she signs. "It would be difficult, even for an experienced teacher, to attempt what is being asked of you. Allow me to look into it? I will write up some notes from my own experience, as well as my research, and get them to you as soon as possible. All right?"

38

I nod and thank her, lost in thought. Can this truly be done, and am I the correct person to attempt it? What if I do wrong, and set the girl back even further? On the other hand, what if I am her only hope? I'm an unfamiliar tangle of emotions, uncertain as to how this makes me feel. Is this mix of anxiety and excitement what I will feel when I am a teacher?

As I'm leaving, Mrs. Pye touches my shoulder and signs, "If you need anything, Mary—anything—I will help as I can. Remember, you have many friends."

I feel heartened that I will not be alone in my quest. I'm certain I will further draw on her experiences. We part, and I decide to seek spiritual counsel. I walk back up the high road and past our house. This time, Reverend Lee is outside his house raking leaves.

"Come in, come in," he gestures with one hand. He stoops his tall, thin frame to enter the doorway.

I sit on the burgundy sofa, and he takes a wooden chair in the front parlor of the rectory. I pull the crumpled letter out of my pocket and reread it. Before I can offer it, he raises a hand.

"Your father has confided in me, Mary," he signs with some awkwardness.

I sigh and hold the letter in my lap. His housekeeper, the Widow Tilton, places a tray of tea and biscuits between us. I politely shake my head. Reverend Lee stirs his cup and lays the spoon in the saucer.

"I've consulted with Mrs. Pye," I sign slowly so he can understand. "She's going to jot down some notes for me. I've always dreamt of being a schoolteacher. Maybe not under these specific circumstances."

"The child's soul is in peril," Reverend Lee signs.

I'm taken aback, but he continues.

"The question is not whether the pursuit is worthwhile, but if you are fit to answer the calling."

I must look offended, because he explains, "The ordeal you experienced would shake any being to its soul. You have been resilient and rejoined the community with a full heart. But I still sense your fear and agitation at times."

I rub the tip of my boot against the braided rug and think before I answer.

"I can't deny," I sign, "that my kidnapping and captivity in Boston have left a permanent mark on me. I feel afraid looking out at the ocean, and the idea of traveling off-island for any period of time gives me pause. But I'm stalling here. My fellows have moved ahead, and I'm still treading the same old ground."

"As tempting as it must be, you shouldn't see the opportunity as a chance to run away," he signs. "You must be resolved to assist the poor girl, even putting her needs before your own. Can you do that?"

"I don't know," I sign. "Thank you for giving me food for thought. I promised Papa I'll think carefully before replying to Nora."

"Good! Now if you'll excuse me, I have a quandary I'm sure you'll understand. A bit of trouble putting Sunday's sermon into writing. It's all up here." He taps his head. "It's just a question of . . ."

"Letting it out," I finish his sentence.

"Indeed," he replies, running a bony hand over his bare head with its scant gray wisps.

Reverend Lee takes my hand before I leave. It's not a benediction, but I feel blessed for his advice. I don't feel ready to go home. Where else shall I wander?

I end up perched awkwardly in the branches of an apple tree that Nancy and I used to climb when we were younger. I am slightly too big now, as the bough bends beneath me, and my fancier clothes make the task a bit of a chore. Nancy is the only other person I would consult on a matter of such importance.

When she and I came here, I would watch her play the recorder that her uncle, Jeremiah Skiffe, made for her and we would spy on our neighbors. She would think of this invitation as an adventure. She would be bold, I'm sure of it. Perhaps I need someone encouraging me to be unafraid. In my head, I begin to draft a letter to my dear friend, which makes me feel as if she is advising me.

Dearest Nancy, I think. *What an opportunity has come to me!* I describe the situation in a way that would stimulate her, describing a remote manor. *It's called the Vale and sits apart from all other houses, naturally secluded. The family is away for the season, and many parts of the house lie dormant with only a few servants to run it.*

Of the mystery of the young mistress, I think, *What has led to her tragic situation, no one knows. It is a secret that I must uncover.* And about the voyage into the unknown that I would be taking, I ponder, *What ship would bear me, and what would be waiting for me when we dock?*

I imagine her sly smile of excitement and it lightens my heart.

I head home and keep that picture in my head when I greet Mama and Papa. I am aware of them giving me cautious and curious looks as I silently help with chores. Watching me. I'm not yet ready to discuss the conclusion that I'm coming to, so I request to be excused. Mama looks as if she wants to ask me something but nods and smiles tightly, stopping me to plant a kiss on the top of my head as she used to do when I was little.

In my room, I sit at my desk and write my letter to Nancy. As I scribble it out in ink, I feel again the swell of excitement flutter in my stomach, a mixture of anxiety and anticipation that's always guided me before. I realize I've made my decision. I want to post my correspondence by the end of the day. I'll inform Nancy she can reach me at the Vale.

Chapter Six

Mama is less than pleased when I tell her my decision. Her mouth is thinly set as she looks at Papa, who nods.

"We'll contact this Miss O'Neal posthaste," she says, "to make certain that she will take responsibility for your well-being."

I step up and sign, "I'll send the reply." (In truth, I already have.) "And I think it appropriate for Reverend Lee to be my traveling chaperone, at least as far as Boston." That brings some relief to Mama's face.

Mama takes off her apron and makes the sign for knocking. I peek down the hallway from the kitchen to the front door. Mama welcomes Mrs. Pye into the house.

Though both are hearing, Mama signs, "Mary has decided to go."

Mrs. Pye pats her hands and signs, "I assumed she would. I guess she's watching us now, so let's call her in."

I don't make Mama come to get me. I lean against the entrance to the front parlor. Mrs. Pye sits in one of the blue chairs, while Mama perches on the sofa.

"Mary," Mrs. Pye finger-spells. "I didn't notice the scrapes on your face yesterday."

"I noticed that last night," Mama interjects. "But I was too distressed to ask."

I quickly draw whiskers on my cheeks—the sign for "cat." I exhale when they let the subject drop.

"I have some notes for you," Mrs. Pye says. "I had an hour while Lissy slept yesterday. I felt you'd make a quick decision, which perhaps is just as well."

"I'd prefer she took her time," Mama signs. "As we did when we were young."

"Did we?" Mrs. Pye asks. "I became a schoolteacher without my father's approval. Youth leap fearlessly, which is foolhardy—but it can also be marvelous. I believe in Mary."

"Of course," Mama signs, "I have every confidence in my daughter. It's just—"

"This time we'll know exactly where she is." Mrs. Pye shakes her fist. "We'll storm the gates if anything goes wrong."

"The girl sounds dangerous." Mama's hand flutters to her neck.

"She's being treated like an animal," Mrs. Pye signs.

I must groan or make some other sound. They suddenly remember I'm standing here. Mrs. Pye smiles and reaches out her hand. I take the paper she offers.

She signs, "There are details that will make more sense once you begin your lessons. I've written three guiding principles at the top. Keep them in mind, even at your most frustrated, when you want to walk away."

I commit them to memory.

1. A person is intelligent even if they don't have language.
2. Where you come from is less important than what you achieve.
3. Never give up on a student.

I thank her, and she takes my hands in hers, giving them a gentle squeeze, silently wishing me luck. I go to my room while Mama and Mrs. Pye continue to talk. Soothing Mama's fears is just one of many reasons I am so incredibly grateful to Mrs. Pye.

I sit at my desk to examine the notes. I puzzle over some statements and nod in recognition at others such as this:

Written literacy begins with the ABCs, but with sign language it's more useful to point to objects or make motions while forming the appropriate sign. If a deaf child does not yet realize that things have names, repetition is the key to opening the doors of language in her heart and mind.

I spend the next week preparing while waiting for instructions from Nora. Part of me is hoping she'll rescind the offer. The manor is isolated. I couldn't run away hoping to find a friend as I did in Boston. What if it is a trick to lure me away for more experimentation? I'm jumpy and overexcited.

I have no travel trunk and Papa's would be too coarse for me. I wonder if a neighbor might lend me one. Who on the Vineyard would have something so fine that it would look at home in a place like the Vale? The answer is obvious, but it makes me groan inwardly.

The Hillmans agree to loan me a trunk, so I won't appear too provincial. Papa says he'll retrieve it. When we arrive, I gesture for him to stay in the carriage. I knock at the front door and Mrs. Hillman tells me to go round to the barn. Unluckily, Sarah decides to follow me.

"I wouldn't be treated as a servant," she signs, her nose pointed upward. "But Father says there are great architectural homes in Waltham, influenced by Georgian style in England. President Jefferson favors it. It's unlikely you'll fit in. Anyway, English loyalists resided there. Do you want to live among hidden traitors?"

"I'll take my chances," I reply curtly.

"I prefer to speak for myself, Sarah," Mr. Hillman signs, coming up behind us. He's an elegant man, by Vineyard standards. He wears spectacles and is the source of his daughter's striking red hair.

Sarah fumes but holds her tongue as Papa and her father lift the trunk onto our cart.

"We'll pray for you," Mr. Hillman signs, holding the palms of his hands together. I accept his blessing for my journey. I hope Sarah wishes me well in her heart.

～　～　～

When we arrive home, Mama is sitting with Reverend Lee. I see he's offering her comfort, and perhaps harmless gossip from the village to amuse her.

The four of us eat chicken soup to take the nip out of the September air. Then Reverend Lee unrolls a map indicating our route. Nancy lives in Quincy, about ten miles south of Boston. John Adams was born there and returned to his farm, Peacefield, after a crushing defeat by President Jefferson. Nancy's uncle, Jeremiah Skiffe, made his money in shipbuilding, a big step up from his early fishing days on the Vineyard. I wonder how it would feel to see him again.

I turn my attention back to the map. We'll cross the Atlantic to Cape Cod. My stomach drops. Can I set foot on Ezra Brewer's *Black Dog* again? I trust he can steer us to our destination. Then we'll make our way over the narrowest strip of land by cart and sail on to Boston. Reverend Lee has friends who will help us along the way.

How will I be treated by these friends? How will the outside world view me? I left the Vineyard once before, against my will, and was ill-handled and looked down upon. This is a different circumstance. They are

49

expecting me; they know I'm different. There's fear, yes. I tell myself that's natural. Might I even encounter others who are different, from me and from the rest of the world?

And what of the girl, her odd behavior and mysterious confinement? She's the reason I've agreed to leave in the first place. What might I discover about her?

With these thoughts in mind, I retire to my room to pack.

Nancy gave me a fashionable black beaver hat the December she visited. Mama helped me sew a black cloak from the finest merino wool. I'll need proper attire, along with practical shifts, petticoats, and stockings.

Not knowing what supplies they have for instruction at the Vale, I pack my old slate and wrap pieces of chalk in a cloth. I assume they'll offer me paper and ink. I'll carry Grandmother Harmony's Bible for luck and instruction.

Shall I bring a gift for the child? Has she ever had a toy? There aren't any left in our home. Before I can think further, Mama sends me to the barn. What have I done to deserve this? The boys are lined up in size order. Their tone is mock solemnity. Eamon says something and gestures to Liam, whose hands are tucked behind his back. I narrow my eyes suspiciously as I approach.

The twins duck their heads bashfully as Liam babbles something I don't understand, and shoves what he's been hiding behind his back into my grasp. To my surprise, it's a small doll made of the dried grass we feed to the sheep and clothed in a tied handkerchief to make a dress and cap. A dollop of wool forms her hair. I am stunned and turn it between my fingers. "Thank you," I sign.

Liam blushes an even brighter red than usual, mutters something else and, after repeating my "thank you" as to say "you're welcome," gives me a kiss on the cheek and dashes off in good-natured embarrassment. The twins follow quickly. I look to Eamon, my eyebrows raised. He shakes his head and breaks into a wide grin.

The doll's face is a smooth, bare ball of twisted straw, and yet it seems to stare up at me benignly. It is soft and the handkerchief is worn and faded. It couldn't hurt anyone.

What else will I need to bring with me? I decide to

leave behind the history I'm writing of our village. I'll miss sitting at George's old desk, staring out the window at our spring as I compose my thoughts and translate signs onto the page. Perhaps the Vale will offer fresh inspiration.

Yellow Leg jumps into the trunk as I arrange my belongings. Mama promises she won't put her in the barn with the ginger rapscallions. I can laugh at their antics now. I hope I'm a better tutor than I was a nursemaid. Can my charge possibly be more challenging than that trio? They only learned a handful of signs from me in our three months together.

Days pass, and I try to keep myself busy while I wait. I take long walks, trying not to doubt myself. There's tension between Mama and me. I think she's hoping I won't hear back, or if I do, that they no longer need me.

At last, when I return home one afternoon, there's a letter from Nora waiting for me on the kitchen table.

Dear Mary,

    I'm so pleased you've decided to come! Your spirit will be a great asset to the girl, and we'll learn signs together. I knew you'd have the pluck to accept the challenge.

A carriage will wait for you at the harbor after dusk to whisk you to the Vale in Waltham. I think you'll be impressed by the house and grounds.

I can hardly wait to see you again. But when you arrive, perhaps it's best if we are not too familiar with each other. Not everything here is as it seems.

Sincerely,
Miss Nora O'Neal

Mama sits across from me. I pass her the letter. She reads quickly and puts it down.

"I thought you'd stay," she signs.

"Not forever," I sign.

"Even with everything that's happened? The mysterious nature of Miss O'Neal's correspondence sets my nerves on end."

"Do you want me to stay afraid?" I ask.

"Of course not," she signs. "But I'd prefer to keep you here."

"I'll come back," I tell her.

"Will you?" she signs. "Even if you make a great success?"

"I will," I sign resolutely.

"That's that, then," she signs, and starts folding laundry. I can see she's gently crying as I turn to wash the dishes. She dabs her eyes. We work silently together in rhythm. I hope I'll be able to conjure warm feelings from home when I need succor.

Papa is tender. He asks me to help in the barn. "I'm memorizing you," he signs when I catch him watching me feed the sheep.

I can't help it. I jump into his arms like a child. He's the hardest to leave. Papa. My rock. Always standing just close enough to catch me if I fall but leaving room for me to make mistakes. A farmer with a sailor's heart who understands the desire to travel beyond the horizon. We're both more comfortable out of doors. I take a pinch of tobacco from Papa's shirt and slip it into my skirt pocket to keep the scent of him.

"If you see Sally," I tell him, "tell her where I go."

He taps his finger at the side of his eye. He looks after her when she comes to Chilmark and will pass along my news.

When the day comes, I don't bid farewell to neighbors, even though I don't know how long I'll be gone. I'm not ignoring niceties. I'm singularly focused on arriving at my destination and helping a child as pitiable as I could have been under different circumstances. Perhaps I fear that seeing loved ones will weaken my resolve.

Down on the beach, Papa puts an arm around me, and I squeeze his big hand. So much said without speech.

Mama wraps a scarf around my neck, tying it in a careful knot, and adjusts my beaver hat. She is fussing, her face stern and sad. Could she be thinking of George? If he had lived, he would have wanted to stay closer to home. To family.

Mama looks me over. "Sometimes," she signs, "I wish you were more like me."

It stings and makes me doubt myself. I hug her and brush away a tear.

I climb over the gangplank and board the boat. Ezra Brewer is not as strong as he once was, and another sailor, a friend of his, carries my trunk on after me.

Ezra Brewer signs, "If it isn't Mary Lambert, striking out on her own! I won't haul you back again if you get your nose in the mud."

"I don't expect it," I reply. Though I'm trying to

keep composure, I stick out my tongue, and he cocks his head and flaps his lips in amusement.

As the cutter sails away, I imagine Mama getting back to work in the kitchen, washing beans, Yellow Leg drowsing by the hearth, and Papa finishing his cup of tea before returning to plow the fields. I stand and wave goodbye to my house and my island. Looking toward the future, but unable to free myself from the past.

Chapter
Seven

Ezra Brewer is jaunty at the helm. He's delighted to be off dry land. I half expect him to leap on the bowsprit. I am working to get my sea legs back.

The waves aren't kicking up in protest. It's as if an invisible hand cleared a path through the gray sea so we could cross without trouble. I take it as a sign that my journey is the will of the Almighty.

"Didn't I tell ye I fear no peril from Sirens nor combatant?" Ezra Brewer signs.

I don't have the heart to tell him his part in this adventure is without risk. That doesn't mean he has nothing to offer. He warms up before signing, vigorously rubbing each arm from elbow to hand.

Ladybird, ladybird,
Fly away home.
Your house is on fire,
And your children all gone.
All except one . . .

"Why do you recite that?" I ask, feeling a chill brought on by more than the autumn breeze.

"'Tis true, 'tis not?" he signs.

"What's true?" I sign.

"The gal you're going to teach," he signs. "She's the only one—the family's run away, leaving her alone."

"You don't know anything about her!" I insist.

"No more than you," he signs.

. . . She has crept under
The warming pan.

"Stop it!" I shake my hands in the air.

Reverend Lee soothes, "It's just a familiar rhyme, Mary. I don't see any particular relevance to your noble crusade."

Ezra Brewer throws back his head in laughter. Blasphemy! Before I can reprimand him, and demand to know his full meaning, my chaperone intervenes.

Reverend Lee signs, "I thought you had a black cat for a companion."

Ezra Brewer assures us, "She's still kicking around. An old curiosity, like me." He points to Smithy leaning over the bow. Her one eye is rheumy. Is she looking to catch a fish or just batting the reflection of clouds on the water?

"Why are you trying to frighten me?" I sign. I know Ezra Brewer is needling me, but I can't easily let go. "I thought you said the time is for the young."

He gives me a sideways glance for throwing his words back at him.

"During your captivity," Ezra Brewer signs, opening and closing his hands to keep his fingers pliable, "did you ever scream? Rising from your chest, working the tight cords in your throat, flapping your little-used tongue?"

"What's your meaning?" I sign as my chaperone looks on nervously.

"Your pa told me the girl gasps and clicks. There's no remedy. She's lost."

I sign, "You would give up on one such as us, only denied the sense of sound? A child no less."

"A beast," he replies.

I gasp. Reverend Lee holds me against his chest.

"Horrible," I sign, flicking the fingers on both hands in his direction.

Ezra Brewer's blue eyes darken to the pitch of a midnight sky. "Do you think, girlie, you're the first to try? The only one who's been told a tale of woe? Who's looked for a spark, even kinship in a soul silenced not by nature, but from rejection the moment she passed through the womb, unexpected in her strangeness?"

Reverend Lee recites John 1:5. "The light shines in the darkness, and the darkness has not overcome it."

This calms me. I tell Ezra Brewer, "You don't know everything."

"Nay," he signs, "and I make it my mission to forewarn all. Specially those I care for."

"I will succeed," I tell him.

"I give you credit," he admits.

"The Lord goes with our Mary," Reverend Lee signs.

At that, it begins to rain—a curtain of lace, but nevertheless dampening. Ezra Brewer rolls his eyes skyward and cackles. I squint and glimpse land in the distance.

As we beach in Barnstable County, I uncross my arms. I pet finicky Smithy, and I graze Ezra Brewer's shoulder with my fingertips. I wish to express my gratitude without getting into another spat. Once that's done, Reverend Lee and I climb out of the boat.

"Will you be all right sailing back to the Vineyard on your own?" Reverend Lee signs. "Go easy, Ezra."

"You go easy!" Ezra Brewer signs, waving an arm in front of his face like he's battling an invisible combatant. "The *Dog* will guide me and my first mate back where we belong, full tilt. It's you who ought to mind your way."

I turn my back to him and walk up the rocky beach. A man walks past me, and I wait by his oxcart in the road. Soon he carries the trunk to the cart with Reverend Lee talking animatedly by his side. I pat the two enormous animals hitched in front, having to reach to touch their muzzles, then climb into the seat. I turn back to see Reverend Lee praying with the farmer. The fellow tips his hat and off we go.

The landscape of the Cape is similar to the Vineyard. We pass sand dunes and pitch pines. Reverend Lee is accustomed to driving a handsome trap. The oxen won't follow his commands. He's not a farmer, and they may resent lugging my trunk. As he veers off the lane toward a cranberry bog, I grasp the reins and pull them toward me. He nods with gratitude, then mostly follows a straight path. His humble bearing and black robes assure me we'll be treated fairly wherever we pass.

Reverend Lee can't sign as he steers, so I concentrate on the task that lies ahead. I imagine my charge in elegant dress but unable to communicate. I think about the two letters from Nora. They said so little. How did she discover Ladybird is deaf? That's what I'll call the girl until I discover her true name. How many signs has Nora taught her? I have many more to help her describe her world. I have only to follow Mrs. Pye's instructions and set Ladybird free the way Sally rescued me from the incoming tide.

The cart's wheels lull me. I am pulled back into distant memory. I'm barely aware my hands are making signs as I vividly recall an old scene. I must have been five years old. It was winter, and I was playing in the snow in the yard. I wandered off, collecting stones to throw at the ice.

"Papa, I saw a man throw a sack into the frozen brook," I sign frantically after racing inside. "You must grab before it sinks."

Before Papa can pull on his boots, I run out again. I'm too panicked to feel the cold. I slip and fall on the icy bridge. The brook is too shallow for me to go under. I crawl and feel all around me. The water is moving, swiftly carrying dead twigs and leaves. I find the bag caught on a hanging branch. I clutch it as Papa's strong arms haul me up.

He lays me on the hearth rug. Mama runs for blankets. George stands stock-still. I'm trembling too much to work my fingers. I shriek between gasps.

George understands my plea and wrests the bag from my hands. He turns his back to me. I writhe and see him handle something gently. He puts it down next to him. A cold stone. Then another and another. Until the last—a small black ball of fur who tries to lift her head.

Mama wraps her in a clean towel and puts her in my hands. She brings a pap in a saucer. The kitten opens her one eye. I breathe warm air gently on her head.

The disfigured runt of the litter. Somehow, she stuck and caught on the bank. She grows quickly, never fully belonging to me. Mama lets her out one spring day, and when she doesn't come back, I cry.

Till Papa signs, "I saw the cat riding on the shoulder of my friend Ezra Brewer. And you'll never guess it,

Mary. She chases the surf and explores his boat." I smile, thinking that she was the only one left all alone, and I helped her survive till she found her way home.

Reverend Lee touches my hand, and I realize we've stopped riding. "Mary," he signs, wiping his eyes, "you're a rare soul of charity."

"But isn't charity looking down on others," I sign, "and feeding them crumbs so you will be admired?"

"You sound like our friend Ezra Brewer," he signs, making me wince. "Well, yes, I suppose some of our well-to-do neighbors may act out of selfish impulses. I can't condemn them, because they're still doing good."

"I know there's vanity in believing that I'm the only one who can reach this miserable girl," I sign, "and I've dreamt of receiving praise for my success."

"That's perfectly natural," he signs, with a gentle smile. "That you examine your intentions is a sign of virtue."

I nod, then almost retch when I see Cape Cod Bay on the horizon. I climb off the cart and put my head between my knees. "Stay in the present," I urge myself. "Andrew Noble's bones are scattered on the seabed and can harm you no more."

I take deep breaths until I can stand upright.

A local farmer will return the cart and oxen to their owner. Reverend Lee talks without signing to a man dressed as a sailor. I compose myself as they walk toward me.

"Mary Lambert," Reverend Lee signs and speaks, "I'd like you to meet Captain Martin. As a favor to the Church, he'll take us up the coast to the harbor."

"Good day," I sign, with a curtsy. Reverend Lee interprets for me. It's the first time I'm conversing with a mainlander since my ordeal. I look him directly in the eye. I cannot unblock my ears. But if I am to be a tutor at a manor, I must attempt to gain respect.

Captain Martin's narrowed eyes show curiosity, but he takes my hand and says, "How do?"

I exhale and smile. Captain Martin and the farmer carry my trunk past cornfields and downhill to a beach with variegated rocks and pebbles of every size. They put it on the captain's whaleboat. Something catches my eye. I reach down and place a smooth black stone with white markings into my cloak pocket. Turning it between my fingers focuses me.

The vessel is pointed at both ends. I pull my cloak

tightly around me and sit on a thwart. The captain takes up the steering oar. Reverend Lee seizes a pair of oars. I am not expected to row, but I hold on to the nearest paddle. We're not carrying heavy cargo, and we'll stay close to the shoreline.

With our backs turned to each other, there's no chance to sign. I can't read the occasional glance or body language either. By the set of their shoulders and the way the boat rocks, I feel Captain Martin and Revered Lee are speaking to each other.

I'm almost there, I think. Will Nora ride with me in the carriage? I packed the slate and chalk on top, in case I need them to communicate. Nora picked up sign language quickly in the past. Her eagerness makes her a successful pupil. What of my charge? I imagine her with raven hair. Will she be put to bed or kept awake until I arrive? A burst of excitement runs through me like lightning.

Entering Boston Harbor, I feel queasy again. Last time I arrived a prisoner on Andrew's schooner, I was covered in filth and nearly frozen. While I was dazzled by the sights around me, it felt a dangerous place. And I an unwelcome visitor. I may still be a country mouse, but I have the deportment of a young lady.

I'm distracted by a struggle on the deck of another ship leaving the harbor. They're passing as if in a hurry. I whip my head around to get a better look. A man herds several others in front of him. They are wrapped in blankets, so I can't make them out. They shuffle and stumble. Are their feet made of lead?

Reverend Lee is watching too. "Shackles?" I sign, my wrists pressed together with a twist of agony on my face.

"They must be prisoners," he signs too quickly. I notice him touch the cross at his breast.

I sign in horror, "What if they were snatched from freedom? It could be . . . slave catchers!"

Thomas Richards, our old farmhand, shared stories with George and me about being human cargo in the hold of a ship with hundreds of other Africans, shivering from fear and sickness. He was eventually freed through manumission, but risks recapture on whaling ships. The first colonizers to the Vineyard sold the Wampanoag into slavery, even girls like Sally. Many townsfolk stubbornly hold to the notion that our deaf community founder and my great-great-grandfather,

Jonathan Lambert, was brigantine on the ship *Tyral* to return prisoners from Quebec to America. In truth, he was selling freedmen back into the bondage they escaped. None of us are innocent.

It's not the same magnitude of evil, but had the events of three years past turned differently, I could easily have fallen back into the cruel grasp of Andrew Noble rather than the warm embrace of Ezra Brewer on a wharf not far from here.

I stand and nearly tip our vessel in agitation, feeling helpless to aid those poor souls. They're sailing far away now. Captain Martin focuses his inquisitive eyes on me and points ahead to where we'll dock.

Dastardly city!

Part
Two

Chapter Eight

A town coach waits for me. It's the most elegant carriage I've ever seen. It has smooth glass windows on every side, and curling gold filigree decorating the outside, like sculpted waves against the neat whitewash of the exterior. It makes the other coaches I saw while held captive in Boston look like plain horse carts.

There's a driver sitting at the front, reins in hand, and beside him, a groom, impeccably dressed in black livery. I'm disappointed Nora isn't here. The groom must ask for me as he stands down from the driver's seat because Reverend Lee straightens his back and signs as he speaks, "This is she." In turn, he fingerspells the men's names for me.

Stephen replies and moves to retrieve my chest, fastening it to the coach's boot. He strides to the door and opens it, standing stock-still like a statue, one arm folded behind his back. Despite his bearing, he gives me a friendly wink. The driver, Walter, stares straight ahead. His ramrod stance and thin frame make him look like a pompous grasshopper.

Reverend Lee puts his hand on my shoulder and smiles kindly. He signs, "A girl is not a kitten. Nor a beast. I believe in my heart of hearts that every soul can be saved. You'll need to learn patience and not to take offense. May His Grace be with you in your task, Mary."

I hug him. My head reaches the middle of his chest now. It's hard to let go even as I'm overwhelmed with excitement for what comes next.

I curtsy to Stephen before I slide into the lavish coach. The benches inside are covered in a material so soft, it feels like Heaven beneath my fingertips. I turn, gazing out of all the windows in a circle, surveying how the landscape looks almost unreal, like a large, colorful painting.

The coach jolts forward, and the sense of move-ment, of watching the world through those windows, is strange, even magical. I relax my eyes, and the scenery begins to blur, a cold and muted green framed by the windows' padded sill.

My fingers move quickly, unembarrassed because

no one sees me. "I've come this far—there's no turning back. Mrs. Pye was once a novice. If I am not ready for the task, I will have to learn quickly. Will Ladybird understand we are the same?"

We turn down the long drive to the Vale. I feel the horses slow from a gallop to a trot. I strain to glimpse the house, which is indeed sunk in a vale. The silver moon makes it glow an eerie white. The elegant structure is a large block, balanced by smaller wings on each side. Its many windows and front door are symmetrical as a face, with an inscrutable expression.

I take a breath as I prepare for our arrival. I've thought long and hard how I'd have done things differently in captivity knowing what I now know. I learned that first impressions are critical. With the deaf, they may determine your success. People are curious. It's best to mimic them at first, to put them at ease. I'll try to make no odd sounds, nor sign quickly, till they've summed me up.

When we come to a halt, I slowly exhale, then arrange my hat and lift my chin. I wear a modest smile.

Stephen takes my hand as I step off the coach. Walter never glances at me. I catch sight of movement in a window on the third story. Is someone spying on me? Stephen touches my shoulder, making me flinch. He sweeps his arm toward the entrance, where a stout older woman waits on the entry porch.

When my trunk is removed from the boot, I retrieve the slate and chalk. I mean to use words rather than crude gestures for our first encounter. It boosts my confidence that the older woman doesn't shift her feet impatiently.

I follow her into the oval foyer. There's a window over the door that looks like an open fan with glass inserts. It must flood the chamber with light at the height of day. The geometry of the exterior is repeated inside. The floor is spotless black and white squares with two green chairs on each side. A staircase with polished banister runs upward. In this pristine environment, my deafness feels like a blemish. But no home is without a cluttered cupboard or a loose floorboard. And I'm here to help Ladybird.

The housekeeper drops me a decent curtsy as if I am a distinguished visitor. I curtsy in return, at ease in her presence.

I take up a piece of chalk to write, *I am Mary*

Lambert. I'm pleased to meet you. What's your name?

She takes the slate in hand and shakes her gray head. It occurs to me the plain woman can't read. I put my fist over my heart to sign "sorry," at which point Nora appears. She hasn't changed much; her fiery hair and the way she rushes about are just the same. She embraces me and then holds me at arm's length, looking me up and down, grinning. I have sprouted in the past few years and am now almost as tall as she.

Pleased with herself, she points to her chest and finger-spells her name. I nod, smiling. She spots the slate and scoops it up, brightening at the words written on it.

She writes her own message. *This is Mrs. Collins, the housekeeper. I am a housemaid, under her charge.* They talk animatedly. Nora turns the slate over and writes, *Mary, it is good to see you well. Mrs. Collins is asking if you want to take tea and a small supper or wash in your bedroom first.*

I'd like to see the girl first, I write, then sign so Nora will connect the two. Nora reads it aloud. Mrs. Collins wrings her hands and furrows her brow.

Nora cleans the slate on her apron and writes, *That's not possible, Mary.*

Before I can respond, an elegant and imposing man walks in and wrests the slate and chalk from Nora's hands. He writes, *She's in no condition to entertain a visitor. Today, she was frothing at the mouth like a rabid dog.* He has thinly pressed lips and frightfully intelligent eyes.

"She's a person, not a dog," I sign boldly, affronted. I detect a flicker of resentment.

The man smirks and speaks without writing. Nora quickly translates. "You'd better leave off the idea of seeing her till I say so."

He turns and stomps off. I feel his foot beats echoing. I reach down to rub my knees. They were knocking, but I kept it well hidden under my gown.

Nora is flushed. She writes, *Mr. Norwich, the butler.*

Before I can reply, Mrs. Collins pats my hand and leads me to the kitchen.

If I can't see the girl, why have I come?

"Miss Mary," Mrs. Collins speaks with Nora writing. "You shouldn't have vexed Mr. Norwich."

I'm grateful Nora interprets oral speech without

censoring or prettying it up. It gives me confidence that she'll be direct with me. I take a seat at a plain wooden table of good quality. I never saw the kitchen at Dr. Minot's, but this is far above the High Tide Inn, where I was forced to labor as a prisoner. Here also is a black-and-white-checkerboard floor. The savory cooking smells and amiable company make it more like home than the foyer and—could it be—a ballroom I glimpsed?

"I didn't mean to vex anyone," I sign, then write. Mrs. Collins looks perplexed by my sign language. It's best for me and my work in the house if she overcomes her unease with my "strangeness" quickly. "I was under the impression that I was engaged as a tutor for a deaf-mute relative."

"Oh!" Mrs. Collins says. "It's quite complicated. You see, she's wellborn, but not a proper young lady like you, miss. The scratches on Mr. Norwich's hands and the gardener Ben's face from when they held her down for Dr. Sellard to calm her, well—they could have been made by a wild animal." Nora is scribbling quickly.

"Maybe she didn't want to be calmed down," I suggest.

Mrs. Collins looks at Nora with kind confusion.

Nora speaks and writes, "I think Mary means that the girl may desire more agency in her life."

"Agency?" Mrs. Collins asks and Nora writes.

Nora speaks and writes, "The ability to control her own destiny."

Mrs. Collins shakes her head, without malice.

I write, *She was created in the image of the Lord and should be treated as such.*

Mrs. Collins smiles as Nora reads what I wrote. "That I believe. Even the lowliest creatures are blessed by the Almighty."

But what if she isn't lowly? I write. *What if her situation is her impediment?*

"You're far ahead of me, I'm afraid, Miss Mary," Mrs. Collins says as Nora writes. "I know what I've seen and heard. The way the girl crawls on all fours and those terrible clicking sounds."

I sign, then write, "Why do you keep saying 'the girl'? Surely she has a name."

"If she does, we haven't been told," Mrs. Collins speaks as Nora shakes her tired wrist and keeps writing. "I suppose she must have one. But I can't imagine such a creature was baptized in a holy place."

My blood is rising. Attempting tolerance, I sign, then write, "Why do you think Nora asked permission to call me here, Mrs. Collins?" Nora translates between us.

"I suppose so the girl should learn some of those gestures to tell us if she is hungry or in pain."

"Do you believe that's all she's capable of?" I sign, then write.

"What else?" Mrs. Collins says. That one Nora can sign with a shrug.

Can I be angry at the harm that comes from ignorance? In truth, I have not witnessed the state of the girl's existence.

"When can I see her for myself?" I sign, then write.

"I'm afraid you haven't made a good impression on Mr. Norwich," Mrs. Collins observes.

"Maybe, maybe not," Nora speaks and signs, weighing an invisible object in her hands. She speaks and writes, "He's observed that Mary is serious and capable. I will try to convince him it will make his job easier if Mary can make the girl more compliant."

"Just a moment—" I sign, raising a hand.

"I know that's not your only intention," Nora signs, tapping the side of her head. Our eyes meet, and I see our goal is the same. I'll likely need her assistance if I am to help Ladybird.

"There aren't many people here, for so big a house," I observe.

Nora writes, *The kitchen staff was all let go after the season, so that duty is shared by me and Mrs. Collins. You'll be helping us with some lighter chores, like folding laundry and drying the dishes. Ellie is a maid-of-all-work. She does the menial tasks, like lighting the fires before everyone is awake and mopping the floors. She's a local girl, the youngest of ten. I think you'll like her.*

Nora shakes her hand to ease the cramp from writing quickly, then continues.

Of course, you met the butler, Mr. Norwich. He was a ranking officer in the War for Independence. Walter is the livery driver. He's quite devoted to Mr. Norwich. If you tell him something, you've told them both. Stephen is the groom. You may have noticed he's less formal than Walter. They're nearly opposites. You won't see him much, as he's in the stables tending to the horses. I hope you'll meet our gardener, Ben. I told him about you, and, well, he's quite sympathetic under his rough exterior.

I nod, trying to take it all in. I smile graciously at Mrs. Collins and thank her for the tea, bringing the fingertips of my open right hand down from my chin. She doesn't repeat the sign. She seems relieved to return to her duties as Nora leads me to my bedchamber.

I'm staying on the second floor. The furniture is fine, but less ostentatious than at Dr. Minot's home and office on Beacon Hill. This must be the style that Sarah Hillman described. There's a cornice around the top of the walls. Does Thomas Jefferson have a small, well-made writing desk like this? I giggle at Sarah's silliness—a moment's relief.

As soon as Nora builds the fire, I gesture for her to sit next to me on the bed. She was my first pupil, so I sign, then write each word on the slate. It's laborious. I'm used to quicksilver sign language, hands flying in their own style. Writing every daily conversation would take an eternity. But cobbling together methods of communication is necessary with hearing people off-island. And Nora is willing to do the same for me.

"When will I be able to see Ladybird?"

"Ladybird?" she asks, flapping her hands like wings in imitation.

"A girl must have a name," I explain, not ready to share its origin.

"You will have to wait," she answers. "Let Mr. Norwich observe that you are not a threat to his authority. Take in the house and grounds. Assist Mrs. Collins and me with our chores. Become chums with Ben."

I nod. "How did you come to the conclusion that Ladybird is deaf?"

Nora stands and demonstrates Ladybird's behavior. She includes some signs and finger-spelling, but it is mainly pantomime. She clutches her throat and points at her ears and tongue. She writes, *She's coarser than you, but something reminded me of the first time we met* . . .

"Tell me more," I sign, then write.

She hesitates as she gathers her thoughts. *When I became familiar with you*, she writes, *I could tell that there was a spark behind your eyes, some understanding. With Ladybird, I'm not so sure. She seems beyond comprehension.*

"I see," I sign, touching my face next to my eyes. Perhaps she needs someone to try to comprehend her in her own way. I write, *Why do you believe she was brought here?*

She erases with her wrist and writes, *I have thought about it. It's obvious no one wants to claim her, yet they can't bear to put her in an asylum either.*

I shudder. *I must know if you believe she'll harm me.*

"It's possible, at first," she tries to sign, then writes.

"I'm prepared," I sign nervously.

I sign and write, "You referenced the time we met, so you remember my deplorable state. I have a chilling memory of pressing my face between the bars on a window. Grasping for proof of outside life. I rarely saw you and lacked the means to ask for help. I believed I was in an asylum. Even as I almost succumbed to self-loathing, I didn't lose my will to escape.

"Every day Ladybird is kept locked away with no means of communication is hell on earth for her. No doctor's powders can still her agony. I can almost sense her frustration, bordering on rage. Her pain at cold rejection. I feel she's near."

Nora points at the ceiling. She's put me directly below Ladybird's room on the third story!

What's the sign for "patience"? Nora writes.

I demonstrate, and then write, *You sound like my friend Reverend Lee.*

I have every faith in you, Nora writes and then signs with some fumbling, "Come find me in the kitchen tomorrow morning. I'll explain our daily routine. Good night."

"Night," I sign.

After she exits, I wash at the basin and lie on the bed thinking. Patience. Not for the oppressor, but for the oppressed. Mr. Norwich has not shaken my resolve. I will find a way to teach Ladybird unencumbered. I will not dally. When a child's mind is imprisoned without words, her soul is not at rest. If what I've been told is even half-true, the girl may be more despairing than I was in Boston. This is far from what I was expecting.

I stare at the ceiling, my candle melting to a stub. My right hand rests on Grandmother Harmony's Bible. I don't need to open it to remember Galatians 6:2: "Bear ye one another's burdens."

Chapter Nine

As I dress the next morning, I tuck the doll in my pocket along with the beach stone I picked up on the Cape. These could be useful in a lesson. Why should I wait a day longer to meet my charge? Mrs. Pye would cheer me on.

I meet Mr. Norwich in the foyer. I am coolly cordial with him. I will do my best to win him over until I'm allowed to see Ladybird. I curtsy and tilt my head in question. He points to the left, and I nod.

There are covered pathways leading from the main house to the two separate wings. I walk west toward the kitchen. I promised Nora I'd check in with her first thing, but change my mind. It couldn't hurt to take one of my walks and find her afterward.

I return to the main house, then cross the covered path on the east side. I peer into the ballroom. It's closed for the season. But even with sheets covering chairs and dim shafts of light peeking through the windows, it sparks my imagination. I believe the word "grandeur" was created for such a setting. I recall our country dances at the Chilmark Meeting House. It took me a few tries to learn the steps and not bump into other dancers, but it was exhilarating.

I step out in front of the house and look up at the third-floor window, the one over mine, where I saw movement—Ladybird's cage. We're so close, but the distance feels immense. I walk behind the east wing. The Federal-style house is designed so the third story is smaller than the first two. Is there a way up to the window?

I am distracted by a most peculiar building down a path of level, round stones laid into the dirt. It looks like a small palace made of the clearest windows I have ever seen, with a curved roof that tops out in a white spire. I spy bright greenery inside.

Nora will be waiting for me, and though I am drawn to this place, I mustn't dally, not on my very first day.

The kitchen is warm and inviting in the chill of the morning. Mrs. Collins is kneading the day's bread with her strong arms, and it must be Ellie who cleans the counters with a rag.

Generously, Nora doesn't scold me for my

tardiness. Mrs. Collins rubs her joints as she takes a chair at the table, and I can tell by her demeanor that she's complaining about the weather. We breakfast on cold sausages, biscuits, and tea.

Ellie joins us but doesn't sit. She's thin as a rake and has a cleft lip. She nods but tries not to stare. Am I the first sign language speaker she's met? She seems curious rather than appalled. When I return the gesture, she cups her hand over her mouth. I understand the impulse too well, the futile effort to conceal differences.

Mr. Norwich appears in the doorway, seemingly aware that the kitchen is not his domain, but still wanting to play lord of the manor and keep a keen eye on me.

Thankfully for all, he takes his tea and leaves. I'm sure my deafness disgusts him, but that's typical away from the Vineyard. Changing his mind is not my purpose. While he's suspicious of me and my motives, he doesn't see me as a threat yet. That's to my advantage.

When we're finished, Nora leads me to a small yard where garments are hanging, cold and stiff from the weather, but dried. I know the work well and I don't need to be prompted on how to unclip the linens from the line and fold them and tuck them into a basket that Nora has brought.

We can't use the slate and chalk, so we work in silence. I point and teach signs, a game she's enjoyed since we first met. Though not learned like George, Nora shares his faculty for deftly picking up languages. I wonder if she's fluent in Irish.

I follow her upstairs to the cupboard, where we place the linens among cedar mothballs. She leads me on a few more chores that take up the morning but do not distract my mind. I pay attention to where we are going, and the routes Nora uses. I try to think of it as exploring, though stripping and making beds that aren't even being used isn't the most exciting of tasks. I ask her why it's necessary, and she just shrugs.

When we're finally finished, it's teatime. Nora allows us the luxury of settling in a warm, sunny parlor. Mr. Norwich checks in on us again, after Mrs. Collins delivers a platter of scones. With my most innocent expression (I'm Vesuvius inside), I ask if I may be allowed to see Ladybird. Nora is nervous as she conveys the message. I see Mr. Norwich answer curtly. I know his reply before Nora informs me: no, not today.

Evening is more relaxed. The floors have dried from Ellie's mop, and the furniture not covered by heavy cloths is clean and dusted. Nora sits by the kitchen fire and rocks lazily, while Ellie and Mrs. Collins play cards and invite me to join. I don't know the game, so I pass, but I watch and try to absorb the rules.

We sup as darkness falls, and I'm surprised by how hungry I am. Mama would be impressed by how much work they got out of me in one day. I recognize the crust of fresh bread that Mrs. Collins baked this morning; the cheeses and the meats must come from the cold larder. I smile and rub my stomach exaggeratedly. Mrs. Collins pats me kindly on the shoulder.

I retire early, but my mind is working too quickly to sleep right away. I think of Ladybird above me and wonder if she's as restless as I. Does she know I reside one floor beneath her? Would she care if she did? I'm here, my girl!

The next day is much the same. I rise, and we breakfast in the kitchen. Mr. Norwich makes certain to show he's watching. We dust the china and place it carefully back in the cabinets. Ellie washes the laundry, and Nora and I hang it at the height of the day in the wan sun.

At teatime, once again, we sit in the parlor nibbling on cranberry scones and sipping tea. I lift my brow at Nora, detecting the twist of lemon in the beverage, and she smiles knowingly but does not explain before Mr. Norwich comes through the door to inquire how my day has been. This time, instead of querying when I may see Ladybird, I ask to see her before bed.

"Maybe tomorrow," Nora conveys his answer to me.

My patience is worn thin like a sock in need of darning.

That evening, when I feel the house is still, I open the servants' door at the back of my bedroom and look up. In my nightgown, holding a candle, I make my way to the next floor where we never go to dust or change the linens. I reach out a trembling hand and try the handle. I shake it as vigorously as I can without making noise. Of course it's locked!

I bend to peek through the keyhole, exhilarated and afraid to see an eye staring back. I spy nothing but pitch-black. Is she real or a phantom?

Chapter Ten

I need the key to Ladybird's room. Nora said Ben knows of me and is sympathetic. She said we should become chums. If Ladybird scratched his face, he's been in the room. Perhaps he has a key.

I find Nora in the kitchen and make the signs for "sick" and "walk." It's not a falsehood. I'm nearly in a fever from impatience and could use fresh air. She gently feels my damp forehead and waves me away. I dress for outdoors and exit through the foyer, taking the path to the right of the house to the curious glass building with the greenery. If it were winter, I'd think the pellucid place were an ice palace.

I knock at the door. It's a formality, as I can't hear the response. I try the handle, and it opens. There's a pungent odor I can't quickly identify. A memory floods me—the rare orange rind Mama uses in Christmas baking to glaze the goose and flavor the pudding. How is there citrus here, during fall in Massachusetts? The sweltering heat that makes me remove my cloak may be a clue.

I nod as I reach up to pull a shiny lemon from a tree. A man suddenly appears behind a table. He doesn't yell or seem startled by my presence. It must be Ben. He has thick brown hair and a stocky frame, with blue eyes like large jewels. His left cheek is pock-marked. When he leans over, I spy the word "Culper" and a small symbol sewed into the lining of his coat, almost clandestine. It's probably his family name and insignia.

I've interrupted him, but I can't say why. I point to the scratch on his face, three lines of dried blood. He gestures in the direction of the house. I perceive his tone as good-natured but worried. I point to myself, then the house, meaning I want to see the girl.

He signals for me to sit on a stool. He pulls off his gloves. I wish I had brought the slate and chalk, even if just to draw a diagram. Signing rapidly will lose his attention. I have only a moment's time before he returns to work, and we are at an impasse.

I remember the doll in my pocket. I sit it against a pot on a dirty table. I point to the table, finger-spell the word and then make the sign. As closely as possible, I make the yarn doll repeat my movements. Ben indulges me rather than turning his back. But he obviously doesn't intuit my meaning.

I try again. I make the doll attack my face, then sit her back down and continue our lesson. Recognition passes over Ben's face. He understands the purpose of my game! He shakes his hands in front of his body—instinctively making the Vineyard sign for "what?" I sign climbing a tall ladder or shinnying up a rope. He laughs, but not cruelly. I pantomime turning a key in a lock. He shakes his head.

My options are few. When he rises to attend to his duties, I bow my head and clasp my hands in prayer. I take him for a godly man because of his tolerance. I pray enthusiastically in signs to the Almighty: "Help me! Make the path clear. Show me how I may reach Ladybird."

Ben stands, and I see he has lost his right leg from the knee down. I suppose he's a veteran of the War for Independence. He must have been a boy soldier, not much older than I. Is this why he doesn't look down on me? I notice he moves swiftly, even nimbly before strapping on his wooden leg. He's watching something through the glass panes of the hothouse.

I follow him out the door and wait as he locks it. With his finger to his lips, he urges me to move stealthily. Ben's entire demeanor has changed—he's become more focused and serious. I creep behind him like a shadow, but I've broken into a cold sweat.

He raises a hand for us to stop behind a hedgerow. He puts his hand to his ear to indicate he's listening. Standing still as a statue, I see Mr. Norwich maybe ten yards away. He's talking to a slight man who looks furtively about him. They shake hands and the man is gone.

Mr. Norwich smooths his coat and strides toward the main house as if he had simply been taking a morning stroll to smoke. If I'd blinked, I would have missed him slip a letter into his breast pocket. I don't understand the meaning of this exchange, but Ben's face is red with anger and he opens and closes his fists.

He suddenly remembers I'm behind him. I press my finger to my lips to indicate I will tell no one what I saw. He stares into my eyes for a tense minute, then nods. He waves for me to follow him to the back of the manor. Once there, he directs me to an open door. He reaches into his coat pocket and pulls out a brass key. The blade is large and heavy, and the bow is a circular pattern. I stare at it in my hand. The key to Ladybird's cage? We exchange a knowing glance.

Before I run up the back stairs, Ben clasps my wrist. With his other hand, he touches the scratches on his face. It's a warning. I nod to promise that I won't be foolhardy.

The servants' stairwell at the back of the manor isn't as well kept as the front. The light is dimmer as I climb. Dust motes float around me. As I move upward along the narrow, steep steps, I pass back doors to rooms, including my own. With the servants mostly gone for the season, all feels eerily still.

If I calculated right, I'm standing in front of Ladybird's door. I feel like a young teacher entering the classroom for the first time. Eagerness makes the key tremble in my hand. I turn it in the lock. Ladybird won't have heard it, but I wonder if she sees my shadow under the door or feels someone is near. The heightened senses of deafness are something we share.

"Good morning, class," I sign, to break my tension. "My name is Mary Lambert."

I swing open the door, and before I can worry about creaky hinges summoning the staff, I raise my hands to my mouth. The stench of feces makes me choke.

For Ladybird's sake, I swallow the gag in my throat, quickly regather my composure, and take in the room. It has a low ceiling and a bed at the far end obscured in darkness. Seeing nothing, I tread cautiously to the small window. Has she crept under the warming pan, like Ezra Brewer's spooky rhyme? I try to empty my mind so I can project goodwill into Ladybird's no-doubt-chaotic thoughts. I count to ten, seeing each number in my mind. Then I feel a vibration through the floorboards.

When I turn, I see an agile figure on hands and knees moving toward me. I step backward, but needlessly. The girl draws up short and falls on her face. Her foot is tethered by a chain to the bed, which is fixed to the floor. She claws the planks, trying to get closer to me. She tries to work the chain loose or pull up the floorboards behind her. There's no mystery in her not walking upright—just deviltry.

I could faint at Ladybird's condition. Instead I plop

down out of her reach. I take deep breaths, covering my mouth and nose. I repeat the scripture that Reverend Lee signed to Ezra Brewer: "The light shines in the darkness, and the darkness has not overcome it."

Perhaps intrigued by my signs, Ladybird tilts her head backward to look at me. Even hemmed round with filth, she's a striking girl. Her tangled jet-black hair obscures part of her pale face. She opens her mouth, swollen by sores or bruises. I detect a pattern in the movement of her lips and tongue. Is she gasping and making the clicking sounds? I place my hands over my ears and shake my head to show I'm deaf too. It's clearly not the response she hoped for.

She focuses on me with some intensity. Her visage resembles one who's drowned. What did Shakespeare write? *Those are pearls that were his eyes.* I'm convinced a spark of intelligence lies behind the gloom. Why should she be different from any human child? She simply can't hear and has been left to rot.

A haunting thought finds me: Could this have been me in another life? A cracked-mirror version of everything I know.

Remembering why I've come, I point my index

finger to my chest, then finger-spell my first name with both hands. Ladybird keeps her hands at her sides and moves her lips and tongue.

"No," I sign, and hold my hands over my ears again. I point to myself and finger-spell my name. Then I point to her and sign "girl." I point to the window and sign "light." Finally, I take the doll out of my pocket and sign "doll."

She keeps a keen eye on me. At the very least, I'm showing her something new. I can't know if she realizes I am naming things, or even addressing her. I sign "doll" again and inch closer to her. If I'm afraid of being scratched, she's more frightened and pulls back.

I toss the doll near her right hand. She seizes it and stuffs it in her mouth, chewing, then spitting it out. She rubs her tongue to remove the taste. I sense a presence of mind—no matter how clouded—challenging me. She's not dim-witted. I can accomplish something here.

"No," I sign while shaking my head. "I have no food. It's a doll." I pick up the wet, crumpled figure and make it skip in front of me, like a child playing. This stirs something inside of her. She touches a finger to her eye, then rubs a tear into the swept floor. I feel ineffably sad, but I'm impotent to express it and be understood.

I remember Mrs. Pye's edict about pointing to objects and repeating signs. "I, Mary. You, girl. It, doll."

Just then, the door bursts open. Mr. Norwich leads the ambush, scowling and spitting out words. I notice Ladybird curls into a ball at the sight of him. Mrs. Collins stands immobile, staring. It's Nora who attempts to seize me. She puts one arm in front of my chest as she urges me to back off.

I am pushed through the servants' entrance to my room. The three of them have accompanied me here. I sit on the bed and sneakily remove the key from my pocket and slip it under a pillow. I won't betray Ben. There's much talk around me without interpretation. It's frustrating to be among such chatterers, especially if they're deciding my fate. I glance at Nora impatiently, yet remember her remark that we shouldn't appear too familiar. At long last, she takes up the slate.

How did you get into the girl's room?

I noticed the back door, climbed the spiral staircase, and the room was unlocked.

Nora shows it to Mr. Norwich and speaks my response to Mrs. Collins. They look suspicious, but don't dwell on it. Mrs. Collins is chattering. Nora backs up against a rose-papered wall. Why isn't she coming to my defense? Mr. Norwich sneers at me and grabs the slate.

He writes, *You are as mad as the girl going up there alone. You were repeatedly told*—he glares at Nora—*that you'd have a chance when the time was right.*

I grab the slate back. *I came to help. I'm to be paid. You are keeping a girl chained and left to wallow in her own filth. When would the right time be?*

He starts to speak, then rolls his eyes and snatches the slate and chalk.

Now that you've met your pupil, you may attempt to teach her some of that—he wiggles his fingers exaggeratedly—*so that she can express simple needs. Try to make her presentable, if you will.*

I breathe a sigh of relief.

But, he writes after Mrs. Collins cleans the slate on her apron, *you will not teach her to write. The rest of the staff*—he glances at Nora again—*aren't literate and might feel inferior to the little savage.*

"My intention was to teach her to sign, as sign language is the first language of the deaf," I sign and write. I sense his disgust at my natural language.

"As the only family member in residence, she is your mistress," I remind him, in signs and writing.

I realize I have stepped too far. He speaks without writing and beckons Mrs. Collins to follow him out of the room. I feel the door slam.

Nora takes up the slate and writes, *He said he is the master now, and don't you forget it. That would be wise, Mary.*

I turn my back and walk over to the washstand. I feel a gentle tap on my shoulder and turn around.

"You," Nora signs, "angry with me."

"No," I sign. "Disappointed."

She wipes the slate clean and gestures for me to sit next to her on the bed. Her shoulders are slumped, and she lacks her usual spark.

"Why didn't you come to my defense?" I sign, then write.

You disobeyed me, she writes. *I'm not upset because*

you wanted to help one in need. But you may have com-
promised my position. That's why I told you to take heed.

"I don't understand," I sign and write.

She writes, *I was lucky to find this position after I left*
Dr. Minot's without a letter of reference.

I interrupt. "Why didn't he give you a letter of reference? I thought he liked you."

Oh yes, he liked me. She won't meet my eyes.

"Sorry," I sign, suddenly understanding her mean-
ing. I thought that Dr. Minot was kind but misguided.
Now it appears his character was as low as Andrew's.
I'll remove him from my prayers.

"It's not your fault." She uses the signs she
remembers.

I write, *I can tell that Mr. Norwich disapproves of the*
fact you can read and write.

I hid that at first, she writes. *Until I sent you a post.*
My ma was a washerwoman from County Cork. She was
determined her girl should read English so I wouldn't be
fooled into signing on as an indentured servant.

I nod in appreciation and pause for a moment
before asking, *Why does Mr. Norwich hate Ladybird so?*
It is a question that has been bothering me since I

arrived, for the girl and for myself. Can he have so much contempt for what Andrew Noble called my infirmity?

I see Nora take a deep breath and hold it, as if she is considering what to say, gathering her words and arranging them just so. *You have to understand a man like Norwich*, she writes. *He started here as a lad and worked his way up. When the war ended, he came back instead of returning to his own kin. He must have been here when Ladybird's mother herself was a girl; I have heard him speak of her fondly. A good servant sees the family he serves as his own. He is extremely protective. He will guard their reputation at any cost.*

"But Ladybird is family!" I insist. The household's deranged mores are beyond my worst dreams. What chance do the deaf have anywhere?

In his eyes, she writes grimly, *she is a mistake. An embarrassment. She hurts the family that he loves simply by being.*

I recoil. The words are not Nora's, she is only their bearer and I don't blame her, but it horrifies me. I sign slowly, "I'm glad you contacted me."

She nods and writes, *Mrs. Collins says the girl*

arrived in this state. Her mother is rarely spoken of. She left the family to marry a poor Cape Cod farmer. There was some sort of scandal. I suppose the girl wasn't born in a village like yours. With the love and support of family and community.

Wherever I go, Chilmark will remain my standard of how a village might include those like me.

"I'll tell Mr. Norwich it's not your fault," I sign.

Nora understands most of it and shakes her head. I nod to say I'll let it go, then.

He's cleverer than the devil, Mary, Nora writes, then erases quickly.

I think of telling her what Ben and I saw in the garden. But I embrace her instead. We link our index fingers in the sign for "friend." I vow not to be foolhardy with the well-being of any of the innocents at the Vale.

Nora writes, *I forgot to mention, a letter addressed to you preceded your arrival. I put it on the writing desk. I hope it brings good news. Sleep well.*

I nod and pick up the letter. It's from Nancy. I read it standing by a window under a full moon. She begins as she always does.

Dearest friend, onward to adventure!

The picture you paint is mysterious, to say the least, and I am certain your next correspondence will be filled with tales of ghosts that wander the halls at night.

I'm pleased for you above all. Leaving the Vineyard was the best thing I've done. I'm invigorated not only by the sonatas of Joseph Haydn, but by the natural rights of women as described by the Englishwoman who shares your Christian name! I am now hosting a local group of bluestockings to discuss the emancipation of our sex.

Mary Wollstonecraft asks, "How can a rational being be ennobled by anything that is not obtained by its own exertions?"

You will toil and struggle to teach this deprived girl. I know you are well-suited for this task and I'm excited to discover what steps you take.

For now, I will wonder about spies and secrets lurking in the eaves of this manor house of yours. Perhaps you'll even catch *one! Or perhaps it will be only a pair of lovers meeting in secret. Either way, you mustn't disturb too many bodies!*

Faithfully yours, Nancy

After the horrors I experienced upstairs, the letter in my hands feels like a life raft in a storm. The reality of the Vale is far from her romances. But her confidence in me and Mrs. Wollstonecraft's philosophy of women's liberation bolster me in my cause.

Chapter Eleven

That night, I dream of the Vineyard. The front door of our house is open, but Mama and Papa are gone. The animals have fled the barn. I look toward the sea. A giant wave is coming. Not knowing where the others took shelter, I run until I reach the tidal flats. I am not careful and start to sink. When the muck is up to my knees, I wave my arms and sign for help. I feel myself sink to my chest. My legs are paralyzed, and I struggle to keep my head up. All that is left above the surface are ears without sound. A mouth filling with silt.

I wake with a start. I must get to Ladybird. But I can't disappoint Nora again. Patience is harder than walking in the dark. Is this how bridled horses feel? Why can't tethered things be free?

Downstairs, Nora hands me a plate of biscuits and sausage. I sit at the kitchen table as Mrs. Collins rises to work with Ellie. I pour two cups of tea, remembering Nora takes lemon. I'm grateful to her, but I'm aware she's my sole advocate as Ladybird's teacher in the manor.

"How did you sleep?" she signs.

I nod politely. I don't want to seem difficult.

"Mr. Norwich and Ben don't seem to get along," I sign, changing the subject and aiming to learn as much as I can about the players here.

Nora signs, "They were both in the Continental Army. Mr. Norwich was a ranking officer and Ben a young enlisted soldier. I imagine that could create friction, especially as Mr. Norwich still gives the orders."

"Ben's last name is Culper." I try to impress her with my perceptiveness.

"If it is, I haven't heard it."

I'm carefully drying the china that Nora has washed when Mr. Norwich strides into the kitchen. Ellie jumps in surprise, burning her hand on a muffin tray as she tries to keep her cleft lip covered. Has Mr. Norwich instructed her to conceal it?

He points at me. I grab the slate and chalk. He shakes his head.

I write, *I didn't intend to take it upstairs. I just wanted to ask if I might bathe the girl.*

I quickly glance at Nora, who smiles. I think we are both remembering how I fought her when she tried to bathe me at Dr. Minot's house. Will Ladybird trust me enough to do so after only one encounter?

To my surprise, Mr. Norwich nods. He grasps my upper arm and pulls me along. I might follow his instructions if he would simply pantomime. He holds a bucket and points to the pump in the kitchen. I fill it to the brim, but I'm not given time to heat it. I grab sweet-smelling soap. Then we're up the back staircase to Ladybird's room. Lugging the bucket with both arms is strenuous, and Mr. Norwich offers no help.

As he unlocks the door, I think of Ben's key still hidden under my pillow, then find myself thrust inside the room. Mr. Norwich snatches the bucket of water. Ladybird has come into the light, again on hands and knees. She doesn't look at me, but her expressive hands start making the signs I showed her yesterday. My heart leaps! Even if she doesn't associate the signs with objects, she connects the signs to me!

Out of the corner of my eye, I see Mr. Norwich hoisting the full bucket. I turn slowly, holding out the soap in vain. Before I can gesture for him to please let me do this, he throws cold water on the girl. What a cruel man!

With a penetrating gaze, she holds her neck steady. She is sopping, but she doesn't scream. She makes the same movements of her lips and tongue as yesterday. I'm not skilled at reading lips, but I have tried and don't recognize her mouth flapping as anything close to English. I look around for a towel but see none. Why does Ladybird not shiver? Has she been so long treated as less than human that she doesn't crave warmth? Smithy the cat is like that—running on the shore rather than sleeping by the hearth on a blustery December day—perhaps because of her near death in the freezing brook.

The butler wears a smug expression. That performance was for me. He's showing me who is master all right. But I dare not flinch. I meet his eyes. I have made my vow to the Almighty.

Mr. Norwich throws down the bucket and holds up one finger. I shake my head in a query. He exits and shuts the door behind him. I try the handle and discover it's locked. Did he mean he'll return in one hour?

If that was meant to scare me, it had the reverse effect. I must make the most of the short time!

"Sorry," I sign.

Ladybird imitates me, rubbing her fist on her chest and making a sad face. It occurs to me that an apology is harder to convey than pointing to things and naming them. Still, there's no reason any deaf person can't learn to express the full range of emotions. I point to my chest and finger-spell my name. I share my name sign, brushing my palm gently on my cheek.

"Ladybird," I sign and point to her. There's no recognition on her face. I wish I knew her name. Does she even know she has a name?

She grasps her throat and covers her ears. Without mocking her, I do the same to show I am also deafmute. That stops her agitated movement. Is she as curious about me as I am about her?

She looks back at her right ankle, then at me. She pantomimes turning a key. I open my hands to show they're empty. I turn out my pockets. She jolts. Her hand is raised in the air—a pale, unmoving wing. It suddenly comes alive and she moves her index finger to her nose. It's the sign for "doll." She remembers!

I point to the floor to indicate I left it downstairs. She pounds the floor with open hands. She rests her face in her palms. I wonder what form her deliberation takes. She points her index finger down.

"Yes." I nod my head and fist, feeling exhilarant.

Squatting, I cautiously draw closer to her. I notice her fingernails have been cut short. I slowly reach my hand up to tuck her wet hair behind her ears and take full stock of her face, which is more graceful than mine.

Before I know what's happened, I feel a vise grasp my throat. What does she think she's doing? I raise my hands but cannot unloose her grip. Why harm me, who's done her no wrong?

I see brightly colored, fiery sparks like the forge in Mr. Pye's blacksmith shop. I remember George's final moments. I gain new strength and manage to roll backward out of reach.

I am wheezing and struggling to stand when Mr. Norwich strides into the room. As I raise my head, I watch him drag Ladybird to the bed and smack her hard enough that she doesn't rise. He looks away as I compose myself, weeping inside for my assailant. Bitterly I follow him as he marches downstairs.

Mr. Norwich barks at Mrs. Collins. She hurries away and returns with Walter, who I haven't seen since I arrived. The nimble man is fleet to follow his master's commands. Like a schoolboy who trails a bigger bully with a smirk. His darting eyes unnerve me. I am relieved when Nora appears with the clean slate and chalk.

They're fetching Dr. Sellard, she writes, looking grim.

I take the slate and chalk from her hands. I'm ready to write a screed. But I look into Nora's worried eyes and remember her directive and Reverend Lee's about patience. I drop my arms to my sides, releasing the tension.

Nora examines my neck. There's some pain, but mostly I cough. Ellie rushes to prepare a pot of tea, and I wait in the foyer until the doctor arrives.

He is a boisterous man who appears more clinical than cruel. I curtsy and he takes my hand. Nora interprets on the slate. With a polite wave, I decline his offer of examination. I could use a poultice, but don't trust him. His interest in Ladybird seems impersonal. Does he lack curiosity about her situation? Perhaps he is paid handsomely or is busy with other patients. Maybe he believes he is offering succor to the girl. Clearly, he's never been treated like a vicious cretin.

Mr. Norwich glances at me with pity and revulsion before speaking to Nora and leading the doctor upstairs. It stings my pride. Nora and I head for the kitchen. I take small sips of tea with lemon and honey. We converse with Mrs. Collins, who pats my knee sympathetically. Ellie lingers, observing our interactions, particularly my signing. She has a curious mind, far above her station. I could take her on too, if I weren't such a fool.

I'm not certain Mr. Norwich will let you see her again soon, Nora writes to me, and she obviously speaks this thought aloud too because Mrs. Collins looks shocked.

Mrs. Collins asks why you'd ever want to see her again anyway, Nora writes, side-eyeing me. I pause to think, my mind reeling, my fingers twitching with thoughts.

Was it arrogant of me to believe I could march in here and reach Ladybird when no one else could?

Worse, was I wrong? Mrs. Pye cautioned that I may be asking the impossible. Even she was unsure my task could be achieved. Have I failed before I've even begun?

I think of my patient teacher. Has she ever had these doubts? Surely, she has never faced a challenge such as this. Would she be disappointed in me? I'm disappointed in myself. In his salty way, Ezra Brewer was trying to warn me of this vanity, though he was less well intentioned than Mrs. Pye, I think.

What kind of teacher will I make if I can't get through to my first pupil? What kind of person would I be if I gave up on her now? I think of her reduced state . . . Would I be any different in the same circumstances? The answer frightens me. Ladybird frightens me. She is my failure laid bare before me.

I catch myself.

No.

She is a person, as I told Mr. Norwich when I first arrived.

I am startled to admit that I've been thinking of her as a live specimen like I was. I must change that. I need to consult Mrs. Pye's notes once more, find a new plan.

Can I send a letter to the Vineyard in the morning? I write and Nora interprets.

"Your mother must be very worried," Mrs. Collins says. Her round, wrinkled face has the perpetual look of a concerned saint. "You've been here a week and it'll take time for news to arrive. I'm sure she'll be glad to have word of you and will want to arrange travel home after this unfortunate incident."

Thank you for reminding me of my dear mama, I write as Nora reads aloud. I long for Mama's comfort and approval, which may not be forthcoming.

"Yes," Nora signs and speaks. "We can send your letters. I believe you have the necessary supplies in your room's writing desk."

I take the covered pathway to the house and climb the main staircase. In my room, I strip to my shift, adjust my shawl and mobcap, and begin to write. Mama will hear only of the ballroom and the hothouse growing citrus. To Mrs. Pye, I will bare my soul.

Chapter Twelve

I feel a twinge of guilt for not visiting the kitchen and helping with chores. Nora and Mrs. Collins would naturally give Mr. Norwich my correspondence to post, and I don't trust him not to read what I've written.

I must find another courier.

I glance in the mirror and see purple bruises, like small fingers, on either side of my throat. I wrap the bandage that Dr. Sellard left to cover it. I'll take a day's break from teaching Ladybird and look for clues about her past. To bolster myself, I lift my hands to recite Mrs. Pye's three guiding principles.

1. A person is intelligent even if they don't have language.
2. Where you come from is less important than what you achieve.
3. Never give up on a student.

I randomly open Grandmother Harmony's Bible to Titus 2: 7–8.

> *Show yourself in all ways to be a model of good works, and in your teaching show integrity, dignity . . . that cannot be condemned, so that an opponent may be put to shame, having nothing evil to say about us.*

I don't believe that Mr. Norwich can be shamed by good works, but I mustn't stoop to his level of conniving evil. I'm not giving up on Ladybird, and I hold to the notion that she is capable of integrity and dignity.

Opening the top writing desk drawer, I reach in back for Ben's key. I thrust it into my cloak pocket with the letters. Households like this are run very tightly, especially when they are hiding secrets. I don't want to cause Ben any trouble.

In the hallway, I realize I may need the key again and hope that my own impulses don't deliver Ben into danger with Mr. Norwich. I turn around and return the key to its hiding place in my room, then pull down my hat to just above my eyes and carefully wrap my scarf before stepping outside.

The ballroom, standing empty, beckons me and my imagination. There are glass doors at either end, beneath the covered porches that wrap the building. Carefully, I open the one farthest from the main house so I can't be seen and slip inside. Guests would use this door to sneak away into the gardens. I am using it to creep in like a little mouse.

It's dim inside, but the windows that line the walls let in enough light to illuminate the large space. A spectral dance is being held here; I can feel the ghostly presence of the past as I tread lightly on the wooden floor. A massive fireplace made of marble sits against the wall like a centerpiece. I dream of it lit up and covered in Christmas greenery as the cold fogs up the windows and the chandelier twinkles upon the dancers below.

Spontaneously, I take a turn with an imaginary partner. I only know how to stomp my feet in the style of the country dances I've been taught, but the lads and ladies who frequent this place during the season must glide elegantly, slippered feet making no vibrations against the paneled floor. I raise my hand with wrist bowed and curtsy, as if thanking my partner for the dance.

At the front of the long room is an antechamber where guests must converse and wait to be let inside. Here the floor is covered in white protective cloth, and I toe it back gently to see a precious rug in riotous, exotic colors of bright blue, saffron yellow, and a pink so dark and rich I could never have imagined the like. The pattern of birds calls to mind lands far away, in warmer climes.

A portrait on the wall draws my attention, and I wander to it. The painting is of a young woman, in the blush of her adulthood. She looks delicate, pale, with twinkling blue eyes and jet-black hair. I sense something familiar.

I search for clues in her countenance and recognition comes over me with a jolt. It's Ladybird! Or what she could be, given another ten years. The eyes are different, but the roundness of the face with rosy cheeks, a dainty chin, and her silky obsidian hair is the mirror of my student. This must be her mother. Who was she? Did she come out to society here, in this ballroom?

More importantly, who was she to Ladybird? She doesn't look mad—maybe it was the family who tore them apart and separated them in different prisons. Does Ladybird, sitting in her third-floor squalor, even remember her mother?

A chill bursts up my spine. The ghosts feel too real, and suddenly malevolent. I rush out the garden doors into the welcoming air.

After quietly shutting the doors behind me, I freeze. Only a few feet away, Ellie twirls gracefully, holding a slop bucket she must have just emptied out back. Did she see me exit the ballroom? What can I do but shrug and smile? To distract any suspicion, I curtsy to her with an exaggerated flourish. Her gentle, wide-spaced eyes meet mine. If she saw me, she will keep my secret. We both giggle, possessing more dreams than most would imagine, until she must hear a voice calling her and ruefully scurries inside.

I walk down the entry porch onto the lawn and keep to the east of the main house. There are sculpted swaths of green with some plants and flowers that haven't withered. I tread hard-packed earth and gravel paths. Even without the full bloom of spring, the landscape astonishes in its order and beauty. I want to touch everything, to experience the textures—rough, smooth, even prickly. Tension always drives me out of doors. But there is too much at stake to allow myself to get lost in the relief nature offers.

I pass Stephen, who is heading toward the stables. He lifts an arm in greeting. I notice his long nose and toothy smile resemble a friendly horse. He seems in no way connected to the malicious intrigue of the Vale.

Moving farther ahead, I see Ben's broad back. He's surveying an enclosed area bounded by a ditch. Climbing up to the top of the adjacent bank and peering over the wooden pale, I spot deer gathered inside. They seem peaceful eating acorns. I pray more won't jump the banks and get caught inside to become a venison dinner. They must have been more plentiful when only the Indian people lived here. I wonder what Indian people lived here before it became a stately manor for a single settler family. And are they still here, like the Wampanoag in Aquinnah?

Ben gets my attention by waving his arms over his head. I follow as he takes a path behind the left wing. We stop in an area where trees have been felled. Stumps are scattered like stools. He looks around but has difficulty getting low to the ground. He appears to be checking for mushrooms. Papa taught me which are poisonous and which edible. I examine oyster fungi growing on an oak stump. I make the sign for "pick." He holds up ten fingers, and I gather them.

We enter the hothouse from the west side. What I thought was a quaint, humid palace is actually part of a larger compound filled with exotic fruit and horticulture. I carefully follow him through the labyrinth. Every so often, he pulls down a branch to show me something new. He picks a fig and hands it to me with a wink.

Finally, he sits and takes off his wooden leg. His face is beet red from exertion. He massages the stump of knee.

I put the mushrooms in an empty bowl, then take off my cloak and reach into its pocket. I'm relieved Ben isn't upset when I remove the letters instead of his key.

"You"—I point to him—"send." The latter sign shows the letter on wings, flying and being passed from hand to hand.

He points with his chin in the direction of the house. I shake my head and raise my index finger to my lips. Will he keep my secret?

He scratches an ear and thinks before reaching out a big hand. I press the letters to my heart, then hand them to him.

He touches his throat to indicate mine. News of Ladybird's attack has spread quickly. I shake my head lightly to show it's not serious. He crosses his arms and squints for a moment. Then he nods and breaks into a grin. We both know that when one has a restriction, whether it comes by birth or accident or war, one must make do.

I point toward the manor and sign "long," asking the duration of the girl's imprisonment.

He shakes his head.

I pantomime the girl's feral behavior, which feels like a betrayal. I spill dirt from a pot on the table and rub it flat. I draw eight marks—Nora's estimation of Ladybird's age—with my finger, then look at Ben with a questioning expression.

He seems confused, so I tap my chest and draw fourteen marks. His eyes light up. He underlines the eight marks. I smile and smooth the dirt again. I point both index fingers down to indicate "here," this place. Ben understands and draws two marks.

She's been at the Vale for two years. She arrived when she was six from Cape Cod. What happened during those early years? It's my hypothesis that she was abandoned because—what did Ezra Brewer say?— she was born "unexpected in her strangeness." But why after six years? And what was the scandal Nora referred to? Who and where is Ladybird's father?

Ben cuts the fig and I take one half. I marvel at the red pulp and suck it out from the purple skin. The taste is like a berry filled with honey. I dribble a bit on my chin. I wrap the other half in a handkerchief and place it in my pocket. That's enough nourishment till afternoon tea.

Ben is staring through the glass windows with his jaw set. I catch sight of Mr. Norwich pacing in the garden. I don't see the man he met before. What is the purpose of his visits? Something about them vexes me, though I don't know why it should.

Chapter Thirteen

With questions about Ladybird's circumstances agitating me, I bid goodbye to Ben and head with purpose toward the house. Though I meant to stay away till tomorrow, I feel compelled to check on my student's well-being, even if she's sleeping off a sedative. I cross the foyer and take the front staircase to my room as fast as my skirt will allow me. Thankfully, the servants' door is open, and all the staff are occupied.

When I enter, Ladybird is rocking with her knees pulled up to her chin and feet crossed. She's so resolute, I imagine no doctor's unction can silence her for long.

"Who are you, child?" I sign. Even as I tremble, I find her bewitching.

I decide to sit quietly, out of reach, to see if she acknowledges me, and observe what else she may do. She pays me little mind. She closes her eyes and traces the features on her face. How long has it been since she's seen herself? She tries to work at the chain on her ankle, then yanks at the bed leg secured to the floor.

I'm relieved that her determination has not been run down. We are alike in that.

Despite the griminess of the chamber, the floor is well swept. It strikes me as odd. It reminds me of something I just saw. I can't put my finger on it. But I feel I'm surrounded by mysterious echoes.

I remove the handkerchief from my pocket. The fig stained the cloth red, like the mark under Ladybird's left eye. Surely Mr. Norwich will not be permitted to enter Heaven if this behavior continues! The girl inhales and a shadow of a smile passes across her face. She reaches out her hand toward me. Is it a trap?

She's so spindly from the boneless grub she is fed, delivered in a bowl without a spoon. It might as well be a trough. How can I withhold the fruit, even if I'm knocked out cold?

I creep toward her, this time on my bottom. My legs have always been stronger than my arms. I could kick to get free if she attacks. I reach out my right hand, the fig balanced on my flat palm. She takes it. She doesn't stuff it in her mouth like the doll. She cradles it in her hands, lifts it to her nose, and touches it with her lips. I knew she could be gentle. It may be my imagining, but the fig seems to conjure a memory. Her dimmed face shows expression, even liveliness. Ladybird eats her treat slowly, licking her fingers when it's gone. She reaches out her hand for another.

I scold myself for not thinking to bring more food. What else do I have? A crumple of paper in a pocket, the result of a futile writing exercise early this morning. I ball it up tightly in my hands and sign "ball." I toss it in the air and catch it twice. Ladybird watches me. I don't want to throw it in case she feels threatened. I roll it toward her. She picks it up and turns it over. Then she pitches it at me. It isn't a grievance. It's the only exchange we can make now.

I roll it; then she throws it. She thinks of making this variation before I do! She puts the paper ball on top of her head. When it falls, she kicks it with a dirty foot. I must be grinning like a fool. I improvised and it's working!

Our eyes meet and hold each other's gaze. I feel a stab of guilt for how much easier things have come to me. In my town, everyone speaks sign language and deafness is common. It was taken for granted that I could be educated and equal rather than shuttered away from rejection and shame. In Ladybird's world, I am the exception and she is the rule. Will she ever catch up to me? Can I accept any other outcome?

She mimics the bandage on my throat and grimaces. Is it remorse? I cannot expect anyone who's been treated like she has to be docile. But I don't trust her either.

I feel a tap on my shoulder and startle. It's Nora, come to fetch me. In my haste to see Ladybird, I must have left the door unlocked. What's the purpose of locking it anyway? I feel compelled to stay but oblige Nora so as not to compromise the progress I have made.

"I'll be back," I sign to Ladybird before Nora closes the door behind me. She points at the keyhole and raises her shoulders. I shake my head—the first lie between us.

We stop in the stairwell before entering the kitchen. We don't have the slate and chalk, so Nora slowly fingerspell the words for signs she forgets.

"How are you feeling?" She points to my throat.

"It's good I speak with my hands," I jest.

"Will you be staying, then?"

"For now, at least," I sign.

"I wonder if I did right by inviting you here."

I take her hand and give it a reassuring squeeze.

"There you are, miss," Mrs. Collins says as we enter the kitchen. Nora grabs the slate from her to interpret. "We were worried you left us in the middle of the night. I wouldn't blame you after the girl went for your throat."

"I'm sorry," I sign. "I needed some fresh air this morning. I helped Ben pick mushrooms."

Nora writes the housekeeper's response: *That's all right, then. Would you mind helping us with the washing? We've got piles. It's unlikely you'll be able to see the girl today. She has been heavily sedated.*

I nod and hide my smile, hoping Nora won't give away my secret. Ladybird is not easily subdued. No one can stop me now.

Nora winks at me, then speaks and writes, "I will find Mary a frock that can get wet and stained without spoiling it."

Mrs. Collins waves her hand toward a closet and says something Nora doesn't interpret. Nora grabs clothing about my size and signs for me to change in my room.

The gown is rough like a sack, and as I run my hands over it, I remember the wretched, dirty frock that I wore while working at the High Tide Inn. A shiver passes down my spine.

As I peer into the looking glass and caress my sore throat, an idea takes hold. Ladybird clutches her throat. She throttled mine. Was it the act of a deliberate mind? What was her wordless message?

For a moment, it seems like our reflections are layered. I rub my eyes to dispel the vision. A fog appears on the mirror. I gasp till I realize it's my breath. The house is having a peculiar effect on me.

Chapter Fourteen

My confidence was misplaced. I've been cruelly grounded. Every time I dared to return to Ladybird, Mr. Norwich blocked my way, and I had to pretend I was headed elsewhere. It's been a week since I've last seen Ladybird.

Certainly, Mr. Norwich must suspect I'm getting closer to the truth. I've felt him follow my every move, as if making a ledger of my actions. Even when he is hidden, I can detect his eyes on me like spies in the very shadows. I will need to be wilier to avoid him.

Days pass slowly as molasses. By my count, it is morning of my tenth day. I stand under the fan window in the foyer, my face raised to the sun's kiss. For a moment, I can conjure the beach. But instead of sea spray, I smell starched linen. Compared to the vastness and comfort of the ocean, the open expanses of the Vale feel strangely hollow.

My twin in the attic is the engine of the house.

I restlessly return to my bedroom and sit at the

desk. Consulting Mrs. Pye's notes, I write a list of what I know.

1. *The girl is eight years old—she's likely been imprisoned here for two.*

2. *She appears to have no discernible language (as far as I can tell). She is quick to repeat my signs but slow to learn their meanings. I don't understand this. I'm offering her the ability to communicate, but she seems to have her own purpose.*

3. *I've been told that her mother was born and raised at this manor. She was once accepted by her wealthy family. It's said she betrayed them by marrying a poor Cape Cod farmer.*

4. *There was some sort of scandal. The girl's mother is rumored to be in an asylum.*

5. *The family leaves the girl here tended by the staff. Are they aware she lives in squalor despite the Vale's riches? Do they know how she's treated when they're not here? Is Mr. Norwich a cruel man or protecting a family secret? What would they make of me trying to educate her?*

With my information and questions exhausted, I hide the list under the desk blotter. I sleep too much, and Ellie delivers meals to my room. My door is unlocked, but my movements are as conscribed as Ladybird's. Have I become irrelevant?

I realize with a start that that's just what Mr. Norwich wants me to think. I've fallen into his trap! He never intended for my tutelage to succeed. He's broken the flow of my progress with Ladybird, but all of the pieces remain. Can I gather them and discover what's still missing?

I must pull myself out of this malaise. I button my gown, arrange my hair, and pinch my cheeks to give them color in this gloomy place. Then I head to the kitchen and put my hand to some kind of work to make my stubborn presence felt again. Ellie smiles without raising her hand when she lays eyes upon me. I give her a half wink.

"Miss Mary," I imagine Mrs. Collins signing as she points to me, "as you are not currently the tutor you expected to be, could you stoke the kitchen fire?" She points to the hearth. I put on an apron and do so. The crackling embers ignite my spirit, and a gust of wind down the chimney silently chides, "Not a moment to waste!"

Swerving around, I almost knock into Mr. Norwich. The cup of tea in his hand teeters as he gives me a withering look.

He heads into the parlor to take his tea by the fireplace. The servants' stair is clear of his watchful gaze for the first time in days! Rather than let myself pause to wonder why he let down his guard, I take off my apron and ask Nora to be let into Ladybird's room.

Nora signs, "The door is kept unlocked when she isn't acting violent."

Why haven't I been told this before? I wonder, taking the stairs two at a time.

The putrid stench of the third-floor room still lingers. But Mrs. Pye's notes say to conduct a lesson as normally as possible no matter the circumstances.

A thin gray light filters through the windows. Ladybird stays in the shadows, alert and attentive to me. How has she occupied her days since I last saw her? Has she tried to re-create the ball and play by herself? Does she think I abandoned her like her family? When I was locked in the hold of Andrew Noble's schooner, I counted the days with rice grains. Does my charge have any sense of time?

Lacking a desk and chair, I sit on my bottom and slowly bump my rear toward her side of the room, my legs ready to kick in defense. I'm certain she will come to me after the intrigue of my last visit. I don't know if she's learning what I'm trying to teach, but at the very least, I'm a distraction from her isolation. At my best, I feel we are finally seeing one another, girl to girl.

Ladybird edges into my range of vision. She also sits on her backside, with knees pulled up to her chest and right palm cradling the side of her face. Nora must be responsible for her clean gown. Her dark hair has been cut to just below her chin. I can see her brown-and-gold-flecked eyes, which remind me of my Wampanoag friend Sally's. They're moist, as if she's been crying.

I finger-spell my name. She repeats my movements. She seems comfortable treading familiar ground. I show her the signs for the few objects around us: "window," "gown," "bed," "girl." I add some feelings, like "afraid" and "hungry."

She quickly loses interest in making signs she doesn't understand and stares at the light in the window.

The progress I made with the paper ball game has dissipated. Why did I allow myself to be kept away so long?

I pull from my pocket the black stone I picked up on the beach when I first arrived. Balancing it on my flat palm, I reach out to her. She takes it, and with one finger, traces its white markings.

"Stone," I sign. "Cross."

She turns it deftly in her hand and then sniffs her fingertips. Does she catch a familiar scent? What could it be? I reach into my pocket and feel some dirt. Raising my fingers to my nose, I remember the pinch of tobacco I took from Papa's pocket when he hugged me goodbye. I feel a rush of emotion. Does her papa also smoke tobacco? Does she miss him as I miss mine?

For an eerie moment, I feel we are sharing a memory.

Ladybird's worried stare brings me to my senses. I square my shoulders and compose myself. Reaching into my other pocket, I draw forth the doll and make a show of placing it on its stiff skirt between us. I steer the doll's movements extravagantly, making it walk and mimic chores Ladybird would have witnessed even locked up here.

When I look up, she is frowning, her brow puckered inward. I lay the doll between us again, nudging it toward her, and wait. My heart leaps when she reaches for it. She puts it on its feet, and grasping its limp cloth arms, she bends it to make it swirl and turn and leap.

I don't work out what she's doing at first. But as she keeps at it, I begin to see the pattern. Dancing! Ladybird is making the doll dance! What would compel her to do that?

She surprises me again when she points to me and then to the window. Not understanding her message, I shake my head. She repeats the action more insistently. And then a third time, slapping the floor. She's impatient, and I don't want to lose her again, so I stand and move to the window. Even chained, she has a grand view of the gardens and the outbuildings. If I squint through the obfuscation of the mist, I can just make out Ben's hothouse on one side and the ballroom on the other. The ballroom!

I turn to her with wide-eyed wonder. Did she see me dancing in the ballroom? What has she seen of it? Has there been a party there since she has been in residence? Maybe she watched the revelers and pictured herself there. Does she make up stories, perhaps about the staff, as I did at her age?

I look at her with new eyes. She has been made small and miserable and powerless, not by nature, nor the outside world, but by those entrusted to nurture and care for her. How could they just put her away, like a chipped china cup hidden at the back of a cupboard?

I stand and take one awkward turn for her, trying to be graceful, and smiling with encouragement. She bites her lip, lowers her head, and rests her chin on her bony chest. Am I about to lose her once again? I think of the portrait in the ballroom and gently take the doll from her. I make it cradle its arms and sway to and fro. Her dark eyes are uncomprehending, so I settle the doll in the crook of my arm and rock it like a baby.

I startle as she rips it from my grasp and throws it across the room, where it hits the wall. Even more worrisome are the noises I can see her make, her throat bobbing and lips moving. She slaps the floor with both hands in what feels like a conscious effort to make me feel her tantrum. Rocking the doll was a dreadful misstep.

I dare to smooth Ladybird's hair with my hand,

but pull away when she whips her head back. Either she cannot bear the affection when she is worked up like this or it scares her. I see we have gone as far as she can tolerate today. I rise and put a finger to my lips, begging her to be quiet as I slip out the servants' door. I hope she realizes I am only leaving temporarily, and most importantly, that I am an ally.

What else could she tell me if I were to show her around the house and the grounds? What else would I learn that she already knows? If untethered, would she run?

Chapter Fifteen

Returning to my room, I find two letters on my writing desk. I hold them under a lamp and discover that they were opened and resealed. What measures won't Mr. Norwich take to spy on me? But the news from home helps assuage my concerns. I read Mama's letter first.

> My dearest Mary,
>
> It's so good to get your news! Papa and I miss you every moment of every day.
>
> Reverend Lee told us you traveled safely. I'm relieved that your friend Miss O'Neal and the housekeeper Mrs. Collins are looking after you. The estate sounds majestic and fascinating. A ballroom, imagine that!
>
> It's horrid that the deaf girl is being so poorly treated. I hope you can teach her well enough that she'll be a respectable young lady who is admired by her former captors and blessed by the Lord.

Yellow Leg insisted on going outside. She may have been looking for you. Believe it or not, Finn has taken a shine to her. He won't let his brothers tease her or pull her tail.

I will share your letter with our neighbors. Ezra Brewer is sick in bed but refuses help. It was thoughtful of you to remember the Hillmans' loan of the trunk, even though Sarah can put on airs. I'm glad to send along the warmer undergarments you asked for. Expect a package in a few weeks. I hope you'll visit for Christmas. I imagine you'll know by then if the mainland is the right place for you to stay.

All my love,

Mama

Oh, Mama! A few strokes of her pen with a cat's inky footprint transports me back to the warmth and safety of home. But I can't ignore the pinched tone. In truth, I am no closer to knowing where I belong than when I left my island.

Pushing away these thoughts, I unfold Mrs. Pye's letter.

142

Greetings, Mary!

It sounds like you're in the thick of it. Do not despair if you're not making an immediate success of your vocation. We all stumble when we begin, and the girl sounds much deprived.

I've read that feral children without language can learn in leaps and bounds if given the opportunity. The detailed interactions you've described don't follow this pattern. Using pantomime to express her needs appears to take precedence over language learning.

It's a wild stab in the dark, but from the information you cleverly got from Ben about the girl's age and the length of her stay, coupled with her (sometimes too) lively interactions with you, you must consider the possibility that she had language early on. You can't hear her vocal sounds—could it be a foreign language? Are you certain the story of her Cape Cod origins is fact?

I fumble with the paper, surprised by what I've just read.

In my further research of the deaf academy
in Paris, which fascinated you when you last
returned to the island, I've read of the hearing
teacher Abbé Sicard teaching a deaf boy of
advanced age by bringing him into nature to
stimulate his other senses. Perhaps you can use
your cleverness to arrange an out-of-doors
lesson?

Persist, my young friend! Whether this girl
withers in the darkness or embraces the light
depends on you. Use your cohorts at the manor.
Practice caution, but don't be afraid to throw
it to the wind. Keep me posted whenever
you can.

Sincerely,
Jenny Pye

I fall back on my bed, pressing each letter to one side of my chest. Mrs. Pye's advice to take the lessons out of doors was just what I'd been thinking! I must plan my next move carefully lest I arouse Mr. Norwich's suspicion. Though if he read the letters, he may be forewarned. But I must get Ladybird out of her third-floor prison, to stimulate her senses in nature, among the trees and hills that give me Grace. I'm tired of patience. Even if I'm bluffing, the time has come to be bold.

Chapter Sixteen

The next morning, before descending to the kitchen, I fall to my knees and pray. "Lord don't make this day go disastrously awry. Help me to help her."

Downstairs, I sign confidently to Nora, "By the end of our lesson yesterday, Ladybird was repeating all my signs back to me and she even let me pat her head before I left her room." I still have the childish habit of crossing my fingers behind my back when I fib. And I must, in case this all goes horribly wrong.

The morning light hits the front of the house first, so it is gently dark and cool, except for the hearth fire. Ellie is at the stove baking. The odious Mr. Norwich is enjoying a sparse breakfast.

Nora interprets for Mrs. Collins, whose eyes widen. Ellie moves close to her side.

Mr. Norwich sips his tea and smiles wryly. Nora interprets his speech. "I don't see why you shouldn't try an out-of-doors lesson."

I make sure to show no recognition that he's

quoting Mrs. Pye's letter. Why is he allowing it? Does he hope Ladybird will run off and relieve him of an unpleasant obligation? Does he want to see me fail?

"Nora," I sign, "she'll need to be properly dressed."

"That was taken care of last night," Mr. Norwich interrupts. "Dr. Sellard sedated her. She wasn't behaving quite as amiably as you've described. But in anticipation of your request, she's been dressed for an outing."

His behavior is odd and unsettling. Nora tries frantically to search my eyes, but I shamefully look away.

"That's fine, then," I sign, addressing Mr. Norwich as Nora speaks my words aloud.

"May I have some refreshment packed in case we want to sit for teatime?" I ask Mrs. Collins with Nora still interpreting.

"Yes, miss," she says, and gestures for Ellie to complete the task.

Ellie rushes about excitedly.

"I'll get my cloak," I sign, trying to hold steady.

"Might as well return Ben's key," Mr. Norwich says.

"Excuse me?" I'm genuinely taken aback.

"He mentioned he lost it, and I assumed you

picked it up so you could gain entry without permission." His grin reminds me of the sickening teeth of a moray eel.

"I did pick it up." My brow glistens with perspiration. "I'll return it to its rightful owner."

Ellie hands me the basket she filled. Her eyes are alive and concerned. I face the group and nod, making sure my visage conceals my panic.

Nora follows me to the bottom of the stairs. I climb slowly and don't look back.

Pacing my room, I count backward from twenty. I endured poking and prodding for scientific research by Nora's former employer. I braved the stormy back Cape on Ezra Brewer's *Black Dog* with Andrew battering the side of the vessel, and I walked the tidal flats alone. Could this be any worse? Especially as I know the girl—not her true name or origin—but we share the experience of being undone by those who can't see our worth because we're deaf.

I ascend the back staircase and enter the cell. Ladybird's back is to me. At least, I believe it's her and not a dressmaker's dummy for a cruel joke. The figure stands a little stooped in reddish-brown attire with a

148

fine bonnet and laced black boots. Her face is pressed against a pane, so she doesn't note when I politely stomp the wooden floorboards. I stomp harder and she turns around. I think I must gasp. How different a maltreated child appears when she's shown the slightest care.

Our eyes meet. Though much younger, she's only a head shorter than I. Cautiously, I reach out a hand. She lifts hers in imitation but does not move forward and take mine. I'm nervous to turn my back, but I open the door and wave my right hand, beckoning for her to follow. I carry the food basket in my other hand.

She trails me as if in a daze. Perhaps the medication has kept her sedated. I feel relieved, yet guilty. It's hard for her to manage the spiral staircase. Instead of simply walking forward, she twists her feet to the side to descend while clinging to the rail. As we pass my room, I catch sight of Nora peeking through the servants' door. When Ladybird and I make it to the bottom, still without touching, I'm hesitant to open the back door. Will she flee?

Gathering my courage, I fling it wide and step outside. She raises her hands to her eyes as if the sun is scalding. I urge her forward with signs to follow me. She looks up from where we came—a terrible, familiar prison. I imagine, if she thinks to climb back in her current state, she finds the staircase daunting.

I'm certain Nora and other staff are watching through the windows. Unfortunately, this makes me overeager to prove my worth, and as I coax Ladybird out, she scratches the back of my hand. It smarts and I probably holler.

I feel almost faint. The impasse is maddening. Relief comes in the form of Ben, who appears at my side with his sturdy bearing and wide smile. He takes my uninjured hand and then reaches for Ladybird's. I don't know if it's his welcoming ruddiness or blue eyes like jewels that appeals to her, but she allows him to grasp her hand and lead her out into the crisp autumn day.

We tread the stone path toward the small, white-spired building with clear glass windows. Ladybird keeps stopping to reach and fuss with her boots. Her face wears a grimace. She does not look as enchanted as I was the first time I spotted the small palace.

Inside, I am pleasantly overcome by the heat and

the sight of multicolored plants bearing fruit. The odor is powerful, ranging from sweet to sour and smelly, a melody of scent. Remarkable for every visitor, but unique for those who lack one of their other senses and must compensate.

Ladybird continues to struggle with her boots. Perturbed, I bang Ben's table to get her attention. Can I make her appreciate what I'm experiencing? Ben is more sanguine and practical. He stoops to loosen the tight laces. She leans on the table as he gently wrests them from her feet. Her face relaxes. Ben speaks, then waves his hand. He searches shelves at the back of the room and returns with a bowl. Carefully lifting Ladybird's legs, he removes her stockings. She kicks at him at first, squirming and throwing her arms out. It's a fearful response, but she finally seems to understand by his gentle touch and patience that he means no harm.

I gasp at the festering cuts and chartreuse bruises, presumably from the chain. Ben scoops salve from the bowl as I look on helplessly.

Ladybird used my sign for "hunger." I didn't feed her. Stiff leather chafed her ankles. I dragged her downstairs. Her face showed pain. I urged her on. What kind of teacher am I?

As Ben continues to care for Ladybird, I am overcome with self-loathing. Mrs. Pye hypothesized in her letter, *Maybe the girl is speaking a different language. Maybe her backstory is incomplete.* I kept to a rigid plan when it wasn't effective. I tried to make her sign like me. I didn't keep my promise to her or to Nora to do no harm. What would I have done if Ben hadn't come along?

Feeling better, Ladybird darts around touching the plants and fruit. Ben sections two oranges for her to eat while I stand by idly. She touches her throat and moves her mouth. Whatever Ben hears, he shakes his head without malice. He can't make out her message.

She looks me up and down. For the first time, I can see the girl without the grime. We both tilt our heads. I raise my hands to sign. And like a flash of lightning, she's gone. Through the door quicker than a jackrabbit. I point to Ben. He taps his leg, then gestures toward the door.

It's my race to run! I tuck the hem of my skirts into the waist of my apron so my legs are freer. I pass the hedgerow Ben and I crouched behind when Mr. Norwich met with a stranger. My boots are a disadvantage. I stumble as I bend to tug my laces loose and throw them aside. The grass is cold and slick under my stockings.

With hurried, slippery strides, I follow a flash of Ladybird's skirt around the west wing. She practically leaps over a paling that I must carefully scale. Frantically, I gesture for her to stop. She never looks back.

Does she have a known destination? Is she running blindly? I think of the rhyme Ezra Brewer repeated.

Ladybird, ladybird,
Fly away home.
Your house is on fire,
And your children all gone.
All except one . . .

Ladybird veers to the left, throwing her arms out. I don't understand what she's doing until I see the first hind bolt, followed by an alarmed second and third.

We're in the deer park, and she's causing a small

stampede! The deer bounce in confusion, trying to avoid us. I dodge them and try to track Ladybird under their leaping, spindly legs.

A stag bolts in front of her, causing her to fall on her backside. I throw myself on top of her. She yanks my loose hair. I shriek and struggle to restrain her. Before she can hit or pinch me, I seize her hands. Fingers entwined, we struggle on the ground. The deer scatter as we roll, each of us trying to stay on top. She wrestles my right hand to her mouth and bites like a hornet's sting.

We let go of each other, and impulsively, I reach for her throat. A queer stillness comes over her. Her eyes bore into mine. I loosen my grasp. That's when I see it. A thin scar running from ear to ear. It's a ligature mark. Made by a cord or wire. I struggle for air and fear my voice will rise in a howl. Who has done this wicked thing? Is it any surprise she gasps and makes other unintelligible sounds?

I roll off her. She turns her head. We're face-to-face, almost tasting each other's breath. I nod. She nods. We lie still in the grass, recovering from our scuffle. The deer circle us as though we belong there. Perhaps not all deaf people come naturally to sign language. Ladybird and I communicate more with our eyes than we did with our hands. Her gaze tells me, "I must leave this place. There's somewhere else I belong. You're my only hope." I lift my head and see interlopers approaching. I squeeze Ladybird's hand. It's a vow.

Nora extends me a hand while Ben flings Ladybird over his shoulder and carries her back to the house. I rise and take the shawl Nora offers. Her face shows no judgment, only concern. Her faith in me was not misplaced, but I am undeserving of her friendship.

We walk slowly together and enter the kitchen from the side door. Nora deposits me in a chair, and Mrs. Collins hands me a cup of tea. The nip of rum surprises me, but I know it'll calm my nerves and guarantee sleep. The brew warms me from the inside out.

Nora stoops and gently removes my stockings. She fingers the snags and holes. Ellie draws near to see me. A pan of water is heated, and my swollen feet soaked. I wonder if Ladybird is being shown any care. The thought of her back in that pigsty, abused by Mr. Norwich, is unbearable. I try to push it from my mind till I can aid her.

"Not her fault," I sign to Nora. I'm counting on Ben to have softened the tale he told of our adventure.

Nora leads me to the front staircase in the foyer. She carries the slate and chalk. I don't desire conversation. I indicate that I can manage to reach my room. There is much to think over. First, I must test her knowledge.

"I know." I tap my fingertips on my right temple.

Her bewildered expression shows me she has no knowledge of the scar. I sigh with relief.

"Know what?" Mr. Norwich signs, coming up behind Nora. He must have been lurking in the shadows. And it's clear he's been paying close attention.

"I know you must have been frightened," I sign to Nora, "when Ben told you."

Nora interprets for Mr. Norwich. His eyes flash with suspicion.

"What do you mean about Ben?" Nora interprets for him.

I write, *I assume Mr. Culper told you that I was successfully teaching the girl in the small hothouse until she decided to have a lark in the gardens.*

"Mr. Culper?" he speaks with Nora writing. His

face twists into a sneer. "I've no idea what you're blabbering about."

I'd swear that Mr. Norwich intentionally drops the slate on the black-and-white-checkerboard floor. Nora stoops to sweep the broken pieces into her apron. He must know of the scar and all else about Ladybird's origins. Is it his job to keep her alive or protect the family's secrets at all costs?

Chapter Seventeen

The rum-laced tea is having the desired effect. I pace my room to stay awake. My hands are flying. I sit down at the desk and dip pen in ink. A list to put my thoughts in order.

1. *Ladybird gasps and makes other noises because someone tried to strangle her.*

I lift my left foot to inspect the bottom. Eight years ago, while swimming, a razor clam sliced my foot. The scar is a thin, discolored line. Visible but not fresh. That's what the mark on Ladybird's neck looks like.

2. *Mrs. Collins, who has been in service longer than Nora, does not understand the origin of the girl's strange behavior. She told Nora the girl arrived that way. But I wouldn't put it past Mr. Norwich to strangle her.*

3. Or was the ligature mark part of the scandal on Cape Cod in the girl's past? If her highborn mother married a simple farmer, what's left out of that story?

4. If it was an attempt at strangulation or murder, how did she survive? I've seen animals butchered. A neck wound is usually fatal.

As I nod to stay awake, something startling dawns on me. I scribble quickly before washing up and falling into bed. The last item on the list makes me toss and turn. I stumble from my bed and pitch the list into the fireplace so Mr. Norwich can't discover it. But not before scribbling one final item.

5. Is the girl even deaf, or is she just mute? Rendered dumb by an attacker? I can usually guess immediately if someone is hearing by watching them react to sound. For example, they look to the sky before I feel the reverberation of thunder. Could I have been so flummoxed by Ladybird's wretched state and behavior that my instincts were blocked?

159

I sleep fitfully, then dress slowly in the early light. I have a headache, but I must be clear and deliberate. I can't take anyone into my confidence. Ladybird is waiting for me to act. It's more than I signed on for, but it's been laid in my lap. I'm certain brave teachers have risked all to bring their pupils to safety and knowledge. That's why Mrs. Pye calls it a vocation.

Ladybird, ladybird. It no longer fits as a name.

As I fix my hair, I notice dust gathering on my looking glass and write *Mary* before wiping clean a line to see. I jump backward. That's it! An all-too-obvious piece of the puzzle that I missed. I know why the oddly swept floor in the otherwise squalid third-floor prison struck me. And why Mr. Norwich smashed the slate. The girl can write!

I must test my theory, but how?

I splash cold water on my cheeks to remove the flush of excitement. I compose my facial expression, so often a giveaway of the deaf. For us, a grimace or gesture tells an entire story.

In the kitchen, I wash dishes. I help Ellie carry her mop, bucket, and other supplies to the back staircase. I

160

wink and softly pinch her cheek. Her gray-green eyes twinkle, and she signs, "Thank you." I teach her "You're welcome." I notice how lovely she is. There are only girls here, not monsters.

Mr. Norwich strides into the kitchen. I pretend to ignore him. He leans against the table and eyes me sharply. My hands make quiet signs at my sides. "Stay calm, girl." How many signs has the butler learned?

Nora returns from whatever chore she was doing. I feel I have my voice back.

"Oh, Mary," she signs, then continues in writing. *I've just come from the upstairs room. The girl is sitting peacefully on the bed. She didn't lie down all night. It's as if she awakened from a dream and is absorbing all around her. I think, well, I feel you must have had a shining impact on her soul.*

She looks to Mr. Norwich and interprets his speech. "The girl is as . . . brooding as I left her last night."

His eyes bore into me. Mrs. Collins and Ellie draw near to hear him drop the hammer. "Your services are no longer required."

The others are completely taken aback. I don't

flinch. "I assume she won't be staying in that pigsty one more day."

I can't tell if Nora softens my words, but Mr. Norwich has only to look at my face and body language to interpret them.

Nora assures me, "She'll be put in your bedchamber when you leave." I don't think any of us believe it, but it is a well-intentioned lie to ease me.

"I really would rather stay and help the girl adjust to her new circumstances. And teach all of you some basic signs to use with her," I reply.

It's a stall the butler is prepared for. "Nora is capable of taking up where you left off."

"I have every confidence in her," I sign, with a nod to my old friend. "But, in any case, I'll have to contact my family and make travel arrangements."

"Oh, dear," Mr. Norwich speaks with Nora still interpreting. "There was something I forgot to give you. Absolutely slipped my mind. Terribly sorry." He makes a game of searching his pockets till he retrieves the unsealed envelope. I take it from his hand, my gaze still steady. I immediately recognize Nancy's handwriting, which floods me with relief.

"I'll reply," I sign. "In the meantime, I'll continue to help with chores in the kitchen and give whatever assistance Ben requires."

"Ben will be sent packing as soon as I hire a replacement. I caught him stealing."

Mrs. Collins is taken by surprise. "That doesn't sound like him at all."

"You never can tell who is trustworthy," Mr. Norwich replies. Walter, who's come into the kitchen, sneers behind his master. They repulse me.

"I suppose that's true." Mrs. Collins's bottom lip quivers like jelly. She pats Ellie's back. Along with their sadness, I'm sure they fear the loss of their own jobs.

"I assume I'll be paid in full," I sign. From Nora's expression, she softens my demand.

Mr. Norwich scoffs, yet seems to give directions to Walter.

"I'll retire to my room to read my friend's correspondence," I sign. "I'm glad the girl—I never caught her name—has benefited from our lessons."

Mr. Norwich turns on his boot heel without glancing back. Walter follows. I take off my apron and head for the front staircase with Nora behind me. I turn as

I'm climbing. She raises her hands to sign. I tap my lips with an index finger and point to my room.

Once upstairs, I close the door behind us and gesture for Nora to sit on the bed. I read Nancy's letter under lamplight.

Dearest friend,

What a thoroughly vile villain this Mr. Norwich appears to be! Though it seems as if your Ladybird has already expressed a desire to reach out to you. Take heart, Mary! Remember Mrs. Wollstonecraft's philosophies. Women are more intelligent creatures than men may give us credit for. When it comes to knowledge, you have always been like a rag, eager to soak it up. It sounds as if Ladybird needs some encouragement before she can understand what you are trying to do for her. Don't let possible failure freeze you!

Apparently, you've discovered more than a few ghosts at the Vale. Not every ghost is a spirit. Some are regrets, some are old fears. And some, as you know, are the absence of a companion whom we have grown well used to. It sounds as if that house is filled to the eaves with all of them.

You are doing God's work, Mary, just as Reverend Lee suggested. Imagine how pleased Ladybird's family will be when the child begins to respond. Stay the course! If anyone is up to this task, I know it is you.

No wonder Mr. Norwich wants me gone. He knows I've confided Ladybird's condition and his wickedness to an outsider. He knows I may challenge his authority. I take strength from Nancy's words. *Stay the course!* But she doesn't know how urgent my work has become. It is no longer about teaching the poor girl to communicate, but about freeing her from this prison and reuniting her with her family.

If anyone is willing to help me to save the girl, it's my closest friend. Her uncle's residence is closer than home.

Nora taps my shoulder. She adds new signs to her

vocabulary every day, with appropriate facial expressions. I intuit the pieces she leaves missing or stumbles over. I do the same with Reverend Lee. When Nora is unintelligible, I draw a question mark in the air. She writes the sentence and I gently correct her signs. If only Ladybird and I were this advanced!

"Mary, what is this really all about?"

"I haven't told you everything," I confide. "I don't want to involve you in this ugly business."

"What 'business'?" she asks.

"Do you believe Ben is a thief?"

"Servants sometimes steal," she muses. "Mind you, I've never seen him take to the bottle. He doesn't seem like a man who wants more than he earns. I must know, do you believe Mr. Norwich accused him falsely?"

"That wasn't his first and only lie."

"Go on." She sits back on the bed clutching one of the four posts.

"He's been hiding terrible facts about the girl's life. I've just discovered the scale of harm and deception. I will not be satisfied till I unravel the secret of her history. I know you can't take this journey with me, but I implore you not to give me away."

Nora presses her lips together. "I don't know what you've been up to, but I surely know men. Is there any way I can be of help?"

I whirl around. "Can you keep Mr. Norwich away from me and the third floor first thing tomorrow morning?"

"Yes." She nods. "I think I can manage that."

"Continue with your day," I sign. "Tell the others I'm packing my belongings. If there are any developments, slip a note under my door before you retire tonight."

"Won't you be down for supper, Mary?"

"No," I sign. "I need to plan each move as deliberately as Mr. Norwich. He's been ahead of me all this time. I can't afford to slip up. One careless mistake . . ." I stare up at the ceiling. She squeezes my hand and leaves, closing the door softly behind her.

Rocking on my bed, I feel the girl and I are keeping the same rhythm. The house was never the mystery—it's just a gaudy hall, an empty shell. The inhabitants make it a body with a beating heart. Their actions and emotions flowing through it are its life's blood.

Chapter Eighteen

Keeping awake, I pack my belongings in case I'm forced from the house into a waiting carriage. I watch my first sunrise since I left home. Life in a manor follows the moving hands of a grand clock more than the splendid rays of dawn and dusk in a fishing village. Is there a rooster anywhere nearby and another to echo his cry? Here are prestigious hills and stolen Indian land, which signify position. "Vale" doesn't only mean "valley." When we say "the vale of tears," we refer to the world as a scene of trouble.

I trust Nora to keep Mr. Norwich occupied this morning and focus on our plan. I take pen, paper, and ink from the desk and wrap them in a pillowcase. I grab Ben's key from the back of the drawer.

I climb the servants' staircase quickly. My boot turns on its side, and I grab the railing to keep from stumbling. Outside the girl's chamber, I stand frozen. My hand holds the key even after I turn the lock. What frightens me? I take a deep breath and brace myself before entering the foul-smelling room.

The girl stands by the window, pensive. She has shed the elegant gown and wears a shift. I imagine the world spread out in her mind to be larger than the one outside the panes of glass. She ran free, and now she's caged again. Is there family on Cape Cod looking for her? It seems unlikely. What mama would allow her kitten to be thrown into a frozen brook?

I know I make involuntary sounds when I'm doing housework or am otherwise physically taxed or startled. Hearing people always turn to look. It's their natural instinct, but it embarrasses me. I look at the girl, still gazing out the window at some distant shore that may exist only in her imagination. I take deep breaths and let out a grunt. No response, though I can't judge if it was sufficient to measure hearing. Is her ability to feel vibrations keen like mine? I stomp lightly on the floor, and she turns around. I keep to my belief that we both lack hearing. Whether she is stone deaf like me is impossible to determine.

We face each other. I remember Mrs. Pye's first principle of teaching: *A person is intelligent even if they don't have language.* I was once treated like an animal, yet I have underestimated this girl. As she holds my gaze, I see brilliance dancing behind those gold-flecked brown eyes. Her bravery and persistence in the face of her condition astounds and humbles me. Maybe it's spite that keeps her going. I have learned that hope is a great motivator, but anger can light fires as well.

I kneel and unroll the pillowcase, then set out the pen, ink, and paper. She stands in front of me. Does she wonder what I am up to this time? I look up, tap my index finger to my chest, and write *Mary*. Electricity crackles in the air between us as she squats and reaches for the pen. Grasping it with her whole fist, she writes each letter deliberately, her face intent, as if reaching for something long forgotten. She bites her lip almost clean through.

Beatrice

Light seems to flood the room. If I were in Chilmark, I'd run to the Meeting House and vigorously ring the bell so that all could feel or hear it! There's a faint smile on Beatrice's gaunt face, a radiance but also a smugness. She has just won a small victory, and she knows it. My mind reels. I have to get us both out of here. Could we hide in the hills until we find someone to deliver us to Nancy's house?

As I'm conjuring this plan, I feel a hand grab the back of my collar. I know who it is before I turn around. I try to kick the paper out of sight, but it's obvious from his horror-stricken face that Mr. Norwich saw it. He yells, the cords straining in his neck, as if Beatrice or I can hear it.

I drag my boots on the floor as he attempts to pull me away. Beatrice screams. Not an ordinary scream. One that's been locked in a box and buried in the earth. A tidal wave breaking through a dam. I feel it echo against the walls. The butler must startle because he lets go of me. Before I know my next move, I see Beatrice plant her knee in his groin. When he falls to the floor, she grabs my hand. We try to run, but we're blocked by Nora, who holds out her arms against the doorjamb. Is she still on my side?

Beatrice swings at her, but Stephen pushes Nora aside and wrestles Beatrice to the ground. He's accustomed to handling horses. In an instant, he has Beatrice facedown with her hands bound behind her back. He mustn't have been in the room before because his eyes widen and he gags from the stench. He looks regretful about pinning down a small child.

Mr. Norwich rises and regains his composure, smoothing his hair and straightening his tie and coat. He's got the paper with our names balled in his hand. Despite his calm demeanor, there's hellfire in his eyes. He barks something at Stephen, who blanches. Then he slaps Beatrice in the jaw, swiveling her head like a blossom broken on its stem.

Master! Jailer! Tormentor! Monster! Nancy's heroine Mary Wollstonecraft would have more titles to add.

Nora moves quickly down the stairs. Mr. Norwich pushes me from behind, and I tumble. I'm mad as Ezra Brewer when he got his foot stuck in a lobster trap. Is patience required at this time?

Nora turns to nod at me almost imperceptibly. Beside me, Mr. Norwich speaks to her with an ugly, twisted face.

"Mary," Nora interprets. Her hands are shaking, but she tries to hide it. "Your trunk has been hitched to the boot of the carriage. It's time for you to leave."

I knew this was the risk of my plan, and yet I'm devastated. How can I be wrenched from Beatrice at the moment we've made our first real connection? Still, I nod, pushing up my chin and trying to appear stoic. I see Nora's face fall, though she tries to hide it from Mr. Norwich.

As she leads me to the foyer and away from Mr. Norwich, she signs to me quickly, "I'm so sorry, Mary! I tried to keep him busy. I 'accidentally' spilled hot tea on his britches." A mischievous smile plays at the corners of her mouth. "And then attempted to clean it up with flour. I told him it was the new, most effective remedy. It soaks up the tea, you see."

Her face turns serious as she stops me at the foot of the stair. "What will you do now?"

"Beatrice," I finger-spell. There is no comprehension at first. "She wrote her name: Beatrice." Nora's eyes widen. "I won't give up on her," I sign. "I'll leave, but I'll be back. I promise."

"The coach is instructed to take you to Boston Harbor," she tells me, and worry is written all over her face. She wrings her hands before she continues. "Mr. Norwich doesn't care how you get home; he just wants to be rid of you."

"He'd be happy if a ship took me on and then

dumped me overboard like a fish!" I sign, sucking in my cheeks to pop out my lips like a fish out of water. That makes Nora smile. "I have a friend outside Boston, in Quincy," I assure her, visibly easing her anxiety.

"Mr. Norwich said something that made Stephen blanch," I sign. "What was it?"

"Oh, Mary," she signs with shaking hands. "I nearly forgot! He told Stephen to gather bricks around the barn and to stir a pail of lime and clay."

I sign "understand," shaking my head to show I don't.

"I feel as if this can only be done with wicked intentions. The manor needs no renovation. Why else would they build a wall, but to hold Beatrice? Or to block out the outside world." Has my coming here precipitated this, as if I've kicked a hornets' nest?

I hand Nancy's folded envelope to a gloating Walter and point at the return address. Nora speaks it aloud and I'm ashamed I forgot he's illiterate. She says something else, and he reluctantly reaches into his pocket for a small pouch, which contains my wages in coin. I give her a quick embrace and wish I could bid farewell to

Mrs. Collins and especially to Ellie, but I'm being rushed out the door without ceremony.

The carriage jolts while I'm not yet seated. I look out the back window. Ben stands with his hand raised, bidding me farewell. When will he depart? And why is Mr. Norwich so anxious to be rid of him?

The manor shrinks in view as we ride. The grounds become a distant landscape painting. Exhaustion falls over me like a veil. I feel a momentary urge to put it all behind me, calling it an error in judgment or a failed apprenticeship. But forsaking Beatrice means abandoning myself.

Part
Three

Chapter
Nineteen

That little snake Walter must be whipping the horses into a lather. Poor beasts! The carriage seems to fly over stone and earth to erase any trace of my just over two weeks at the Vale. We're headed to Quincy. I sag against the door and lay my head on the sill. I'm deprived of sleep, and finally feel the weight of all that I have seen and done pressing me down.

Every time I attempt to put my thoughts in order, I'm rattled by a sharp turn. Images flash in my mind. The unmoving balls of kittens. Ezra Brewer's dark gaze when he warned me about the hatred in some for anyone born different. The slave catchers in Boston Harbor. Nora's fear of Mr. Norwich. Ellie's pale hand covering her cleft lip. Beatrice's chained ankle, her joy at tasting a fig and smelling tobacco. How she fought me and then showed me what had been done to her. That awful mark on her throat. How small creatures suffer as much as big. Lord, I am unworthy.

I fall forward as we stop, catching myself on the

handle of the door. I push it open and stumble down without Walter's help. He walks to the boot to liberate my trunk.

The house is not as grand by half as the manor house of the Vale, but it is quite a deal fancier than the farmhouses I'm accustomed to. Its exterior is constructed with beige paneled wood and uniform windows on both the ground and second floors. The roof is flat with two brick chimneys on either side and lined with wrought-iron spikes. A rectangular raised portion in the middle makes it look as if it's wearing a crown.

Nancy waits for me in the shelter of the covered porch that surrounds the front door. She must have seen the coach approaching down the lane. She runs to me and grasps my arm to steady me. I walk with sluggish footsteps to the front door. Most unladylike, I plop down on the settee in the front parlor. I smile wanly and try to joke. "I'm sorry to drop in unannounced."

Nancy puts the back of her hand to my forehead. "Mary," she signs. "You look terrible. What's happened?"

I raise my hands to answer but find no more

strength. Jeremiah Skiffe has appeared from a side room, and as he and Nancy look on with concern, I collapse like a roof without rafters. I close my eyes to darkness.

It is a long and fitful sleep, not as deep as I would like, nor free of dreams. I think that I wake at least once, because I feel the soft, soothing rhythm of music nearby. It lulls me into a gentler slumber that is no longer haunted by fevered nightmares.

When at last I open my eyes, I find myself stripped to my shift and tucked into the soft linens of a spare bed. It's either evening or it's raining, because the light is gray and dim. A bowl of broth on the nightstand smells delicious.

Nancy sits by my bedside reading, and a big, toothy grin spreads across her face when she sees me blink and sit up. "I thought you were going to sleep forever!" she signs exaggeratedly, slumping in her chair to imitate my slumber.

I smile in spite of myself. "I apologize if I have not kept an agreeable schedule." I've missed her laughter. I'm relieved to be speaking with someone who signs fluently. Not that I don't enjoy Nora's company, or conversing with her, but it's different with someone who knows all of my mannerisms, my shorthand and my body language. Though sometimes, as in our greeting, we sign fancifully, mimicking the excesses of oral speech.

"Forsooth!" she declares, with a grand twist of her wrist.

I reach for the broth, and she helps lift it to my mouth. I drink deeply. It's warm and pleasantly fills my belly. I notice that my letter is folded in the margin of the book that Nancy sets aside. "I had fever?" I ask, noting that my shift is sticking slightly to my dewy skin.

"Slight." She makes a small space between index finger and thumb. "Exhaustion more than anything else."

I bite my lip. "I was tiptoeing over glass during my weeks at the Vale, trying not to get cut."

She frowns a little. "I wasn't expecting you, unless a letter went missing. Tell me what happened, Mary." She helps me prop the pillows behind me, and I take another heartening sip of the broth.

"After you tell me about Joseph Haydn," I sign, not quite ready to share.

"Come see the fortepiano," she urges.

I pull a shawl from the end of the bed and wrap it about my shoulders.

Across from the front parlor is a music room. It's modest, with the elegant instrument and several mahogany chairs, but not even the Hillmans have the like in Chilmark.

"Why did I think you had a harpsichord?" I ask.

"I did originally." She shakes her head. "But this is better for what I play, the Viennese classical style."

"Better how?" I ask.

"With Haydn's sonatas," she enthuses, "the momentum of the player is essential. That can only be achieved to the proper extent on the fortepiano or clavichord. Mary, the music has an uncontrollable urge to dominate the harpsichord!"

I'd have giggled at her fervor in our younger days.

"Well," I sign, my palms facing upward. "Show me how it works."

"Imported from Europe," she signs and runs her fingers over the polished lid, propped open to reveal the thin, harpsichord-like strings. "Made by a German in England. Notice it has no metal frame or bracing.

Sixty-one keys and five octaves. The hammers have leather covering so it's not just pounding against bare wood. It produces a softer sound."

"You sound like it's your beau," I tease. "And Joseph Haydn, who is he?"

Nancy throws back her head in laughter. "I have no beau. Such a notion restricts my soul. We'll talk more about that later. Haydn is an Austrian who's spent much of his career as a court musician. He's earned the designation 'Father of the Symphony.' His sonatas interest me more."

She sits on the bench and gestures for me to lean against the fortepiano as I once held on to a simple wooden recorder while she played. Her hands are large, but she moves them deftly, mastering the music she knows by heart. I wish Beatrice were at my side to feel the music too.

I breathe easily, large inhales of clean air. Doors locked inside of me begin to open as I follow the music up and down. It's not inaccessible to me as some may think. I'm certain Nancy chose a composition that would resonate on my deaf ears. I feel it mostly in my nose!

I watch her. Once a somewhat ungainly girl in unflattering frocks who pulled her hair to straighten it, she is more comfortable in her thick body now, and her musical training has given her composure and confidence. She will surely grow to be as large as her uncle. Her ample arms and long neck give her bearing. Her black curls cascade as she sways. The empire-waisted fashion of her dresses flatters her bosom and broad shoulders. She refuses to wear a corset, because of her bluestocking convictions.

I applaud when she finishes. Her uncle does as well. He leans against the doorframe, beaming with pride. His generosity and support made her musical pursuits possible. Still, his cowardly response after George's death leaves me unable to trust the man.

"Mary," he greets me tentatively.

"Mr. Skiffe," I sign with an equal amount of care. "You have a lovely home."

"And I'm happy to share it with you for as long as you like," he invites quickly. "I was pleased when Nancy told me that you might visit. I thought that maybe . . ." He trails off and looks sheepish for a moment. His smile is sad but genuine. Is he trying to ingratiate himself to me? Am I underestimating him because of our past? "Make yourself at home." He's fluent in Vineyard sign but out of practice. There's no rust on Nancy.

The three of us sit together in an adjoining parlor.

"I didn't see much rain at the Vale," I sign.

"It's been steady here," Jeremiah Skiffe signs.

"Are we truly going to remark on the weather?" Nancy signs.

"What do you want to talk about?" I ask, my eyes twinkling.

"I suppose I should inquire about my parents, but I haven't the heart." She sighs. "Uncle gets monthly reports. Father's grim details about the sheep and constant complaints over money."

"Sally Richards examined the flock before I left," I sign. "Your father wouldn't heed her advice."

"Sally!" Nancy finger-spells. "Now that's someone I'd completely forgotten about. What's she doing nowadays?"

"Sally is doing extremely well in learning how to tend the animals," I sign. "She works not only in Aquinnah but our towns too."

186

"I'm sure the villagers aren't always pleased to call on her, no matter her expertise," Nancy guesses.

"Indeed," I sign. "Your father wouldn't pay her for her services."

Nancy rolls her eyes. "Whatever happened to Sally's parents?"

"Her mother died of the ague," I sign. With Nancy, I'm moving away from following English grammar as one speaks it and deeper into my own language with its own rules. "Her father—despair—sign on another whaler."

"The Wampanoag meet one disaster after another," Jeremiah Skiffe signs. "Soon they will be gone. Just like the Indians around these parts. Who was it? Massachusett sachem Chickatawbut had his seat on a hill called Moswetuset Hummock prior to settlement in this area. That's how history progresses. The Indians conquered one another, and then we made the land our own."

Do I sidestep his bigotry as I would a cow flop in the road?

"I certainly hope the Wampanoag won't be gone anytime soon," I sign. "The Vineyard community is diminished but vital. I've heard they're still keeping traditions on Cape Cod too."

"They don't look ahead." Jeremiah Skiffe paces the room. "Like the shipbuilding business I'm in or that pianoforte I imported. It's progress. Traditions are fine, we all keep them. But what do they produce that's essential to the growing nation?"

I don't have an easy answer. Native people are fighting to govern their own nations. Sally made me realize they are varied. I can't think of people in terms of their assets. My ideas of history in life and writing are different from my host's. Shamefully, out of decorum, I don't challenge him. Nancy must sense my unease.

"Tell me, Mary," she signs as her uncle excuses himself, "what is old Ezra Brewer getting up to nowadays?"

"Mama mentioned he's ill," I reply thoughtfully. "But he was scurrilous transporting Reverend Lee and me to the Cape. He repeated a child's rhyme that put me on edge."

"He always spooked me as a child," she signs. "He was full of ghost stories. I remember one where the sailors buried at sea walked out of the water. Just like that. Marching in their uniforms until they reached the shore. That had me pulling the covers over my head at night!"

"Spy stories were your favorite," I remind her.

"I still desire to meet an actual spy," she muses. "The War for Independence is far behind us, but they say there are loyalists among us who have never accepted the founding of America. They work to undermine President Jefferson and his men."

"What can they possibly do now?" I inquire.

"Any number of nefarious endeavors." Nancy is performing as if on a stage. "Perhaps even assassination!" She collapses on the floor, clutching her chest.

"Too much!" I sign with outstretched arms.

She moves closer to me. "You never tell me what's wrong," she signs.

I tap my head. "It takes time for me to work things out. There's much to say about my experience at the Vale. And even more to do . . . if you accept the challenge. I know I cannot stall long. The situation is imminent. But it must be thoughtfully undertaken. The possibility of failure—further failure, because I've already made countless mistakes—freezes me in my tracks."

"Get some sleep," Nancy responds. "Tomorrow we will have a jaunt to bolster your head and heart. And you can tell me everything."

I retire to my room and hope that the stars of my dreams sweep away the darkness of my mind.

Chapter Twenty

Jeremiah Skiffe's servant cleaned my green gown and brushed the black beaver hat that Nancy gave me as a gift. My friend offers me a fresh pair of stockings. She tuts at my cloak and loans me one of hers. She shares a muff to match the hat. We're going out walking.

I never sense the fresh bloom of spring when I travel off-island, whether as a prisoner or a guest. I wouldn't want to miss the flowers and lush trees at home. Or stripping off my boots to tread the edge of the surf, cold and sparkling between my toes.

Bright sunshine cloaks us as we walk arm in arm, but I cannot feel warm inside.

"The town is named for Colonel John Quincy," Nancy signs. "His granddaughter was Abigail Adams. Obviously, she named her son, our former ambassador to Berlin, after him. The family has a vast granite quarry."

"What's over there?" I ask. I'm distracting myself from revealing my full experience at the Vale. But I know I must share what has happened since Nancy last wrote to me and the events that have sent me here.

"That charming colonial estate was the childhood home of Dorothy Quincy, who married John Hancock," she explains. "In the pre-War years, it was a meeting place for patriots."

"I hope we're not stopping at that graveyard," I sign.

"It's fascinating," she signs. "But I won't bring you there."

"Where are we going?" I sigh. "Let's head back. I've seen enough."

"Bear with me." She makes the sign for a grizzly rather than the sign for patience. The English idiom playfully rendered in sign raises the corners of my mouth. Martha's Vineyard Sign Language has its own idioms that don't translate well into English. Brushing imaginary crumbs off your shoulders with your fingertips roughly means "go ask someone who cares." I learned that from Ezra Brewer!

Peacefield is large and impressive, but friendlier than the Vale. The white Georgian structure has black shutters; a gambrel roof creates a nearly full story attic.

Perhaps it's the farmland and orchards that make it seem like a home.

I'm so taken with the land that I hardly notice Nancy leaning on the fence and waving her arms wildly. A short, rotund man walks over to us. It takes me a moment to realize I'm facing a leader of the American Revolution and our second president, John Adams! Nancy speaks and signs to him. It's obviously not their first conversation. I'm painfully shy when she pulls me over, translating for me and for him. "This is Miss Mary Lambert of Martha's Vineyard," she speaks and signs. "Many Vineyarders are deaf," she explains, "and we speak in signs with our hands."

He tips his farm hat to me. He has the most penetrating gaze. I should curtsy, but I'm too stunned. He's extremely animated as he speaks. He was a lawyer in the early days, before the American Revolution, and I can see it in the deliberate yet enthusiastic way that he converses.

He tells Nancy, and she translates, "I know well the importance of communication." His eyes sparkle with intelligence when he talks. "When I was appointed commissioner on a diplomatic mission to France, I never was able to pick up the native language. Much would have been easier had I done so."

"We enjoyed Mrs. Adams's lecture on married women's property rights at our meeting last Saturday," Nancy tells him. He smirks proudly. He does not strike me as a man who would take credit for his wife's actions, but he is visibly happy that Abigail Adams's lecture was enjoyed. "Please pass along our thanks for her contribution. It was very illuminating." He tips his hat, assuring her wordlessly that he will.

A young boy appears shyly behind President Adams's leg and tugs on his coat. He turns and listens, then speaks in return, unconsciously patting his belly. "His grandson," Nancy explains to me. "He's fascinated by our hand movements."

Shedding some of my shyness, I greet the boy. "Good day, my name is Mary." He ducks behind his grandfather's leg but watches me still. "Grandfather," I sign, and repeat it. "Grandfather. Grandson." Nancy interprets and the boy, beaming with curiosity, repeats the signs, stumbling with his little hands at first, becoming more fluid with repetition.

"There!" Mr. Adams declares. "Bright! Like his

father." The boy's father must be John Quincy Adams, who has recently finished serving his term as senator. "He picks up these things fast!"

"Mary intends to be a teacher," Nancy informs Mr. Adams, and I blush deeply.

"Very practical," he compliments. "These signs are a new idea to me, perhaps, but one you live with as a matter of everyday life." He takes his grandson's hand. "Come along, George, it's time to get back to Mama. Miss Nancy, Miss Mary, it was a pleasure."

"George?" I ask Nancy as I scurry away.

"George Washington Adams," Nancy answers with a wry twist to her mouth. "I've heard him say things I shall not repeat about the choice in name."

"About the father of our country?" I sign, shocked.

"Don't let him hear you say that. The two of them had quite the rivalry, back in the days of the war. You wanted a distraction," she signs. "I thought I'd create a spectacular one."

"You did do that," I admit. "John Adams, who would think! But we *must* talk."

"Yes, about that," she signs mysteriously. "I've invited some friends to tea. They know why you went to the Vale, and for whom. I think your situation will be most interesting to them."

"I didn't know you shared my news with anyone." I suddenly feel protective of Beatrice and my teaching methods.

"Their ideas will stimulate you and give you resolve," she signs, then shakes her fist in the air.

"I am resolved," I sign quietly. "I don't know what can be done, or the most effective path to take, but I must do something."

"We will figure it out together," she signs. "Have no fear!"

My fear is justifiable. If Nora is correct, how quickly will they build a brick wall to conceal Beatrice's cell? How long can she last inside without sustenance?

Two ladies await us in Jeremiah Skiffe's front parlor. One has gray hair in a knot and wears spectacles. She's poised on a sofa, a cane in both hands keeping her upright. The other is younger and jaunty. She tips her head back to survey me while I remove my overclothes.

A black maid I hadn't seen before puts down a tea

tray and leaves without being told. Before I can ask her name, Nancy introduces me to her cohorts.

"Mrs. Hortense Redgrave, this is my childhood friend Mary Lambert, about whom I've told you so much."

Gray Spectacles nods. The young woman firmly shakes my hand. She speaks while Nancy signs, "Pleasure to meet you! I'm Molly." I smile at her brazenness and the freckles on her nose.

Molly jumps around like a bright tree frog till we're seated with tea and cakes. She leans against the mantel as a man might.

I feel I'm an object of curiosity, but not in the worst way. I look down instead of meeting their gazes. Until a foot stomp jars me.

"Mary," Nancy signs, "it's time to tell your tale."

Though Nancy is a rascal, I don't doubt the trustworthiness of the friends she would make, and these two women are respectable, even if their notions are radical. I describe the inhabitants of the Vale, especially my interactions with Beatrice. I take in each of their faces while Nancy enthusiastically interprets my signs. They watch her more than me. I demonstrate my missteps and Beatrice's pain. I halt even when their eyes urge me to go on. I don't like being on display.

I finish by signing, "I must return as soon as possible."

Mrs. Redgrave taps her cane on the floor. I believe she's directly signaling me, then realize she wants the group's attention.

"Mrs. Wollstonecraft wrote, 'Make women rational creatures, and free citizens.' The girl Beatrice is a symbol of all that can go wrong when men have power over women."

"She doesn't have power. But I wouldn't call her a symbol," I sign. "She's flesh and blood."

Molly speaks up. "Wollstonecraft also wrote, 'It is justice, not charity, that is wanting in the world.'"

"Yes!" I nod my head and fist vigorously. "I can agree with that. I have often found charity to be my enemy, in terms of those who look on me with pity and disgust. I can only imagine that Beatrice feels the same. Justice, on the other hand, is too elusive, but it's what I seek."

"What do you intend to do with the girl once you've gotten her away from that dreadful place?"

Nancy interprets for Molly, who faces me.

"I haven't thought it through, exactly," I admit. "I can't bring her to the Vineyard with me. That would be kidnapping. I suppose I envisioned bringing her to a safe place such as this, and then inquiring about possible relations on Cape Cod."

"You can't bring her here," Nancy signs abruptly.

"It wasn't an assumption," I tell her. "I'm just not sure . . . I want to help her find home."

"Ambitious," Mrs. Redgrave states. She doesn't look at me at all. I feel the urge to stand in front of her while Nancy is interpreting. "But we do not find homes for wayward girls, let alone those without all their faculties."

"What exactly do you do?" I sign. "What is a bluestocking anyway?"

Molly jumps in. "That's a humorous story. A lady was turned away from a literary meeting in England because of her informal attire. Her response was 'Don't mind dress. Come in your blue stockings!'"

I smile, but it fades. "I can't do this alone," I plead with my eyes as much as my hands. "Won't you join me?"

"How soon?" Molly asks. "I have business in town for the next few days. But by golly, I'd be happy to help you storm the drawbridge and slay that dragon of a butler. A girl in chains makes my blood boil."

Mrs. Redgrave sits still as a statue. Jeremiah Skiffe, who has been observing the meeting from the doorway, takes the floor.

"I think I may have a plan," he speaks and signs. "Ladies"—he points to Nancy and me—"you will play a crucial part. Don't be embarrassed to use my position and sex to vex this butler. I welcome the opportunity to be of use in the cause."

I don't believe he's mocking us, but I wonder why he's eager to help. His intrusion has taken the air out of the bellows. We drink our tea politely. Though Molly winks at me over her cup.

When the maid returns to take the tray, I try to meet her eyes.

"Her name?" I ask Nancy.

"Sissy," she finger-spells.

"That's not her name," I sign. "That's an old slave name."

Nancy shrugs. She interprets for Mrs. Redgrave

when she takes my hands before departing in an elegant coach. "It's admirable a person such as yourself is trying to help a lost girl." My body stiffens, and I clench my jaw.

"She meant well," Nancy signs afterward. "She hasn't met a signing person before."

"You mean a deaf person."

"I suppose so," she signs. "What difference does it make?"

"To you and me, little or nothing. But the rest of the world thinks otherwise."

"I haven't noticed," she signs.

"Well, you wouldn't, would you?" We both laugh to release the tension.

"I like Molly," I assure her. "And I'm glad your uncle is on my side."

"Our side," she corrects.

"Our side, then," I sign. "But most of all, Beatrice's side."

I realize I do know why he's doing this. He wants to put his accounts in order. If this dangerous endeavor is successful, I will consider his debt to my family paid in full. He apologized for the accident to Papa but never to Mama or me. Whatever his motives, I don't think I've ever wanted anything as much as Beatrice's liberty. Even with my erratic teaching methods, I finally earned her trust. I hope she isn't losing hope that I'll return for her.

Chapter Twenty-One

After lunch, we sit in the parlor and concoct our plan. "House, draw," Jeremiah Skiffe signs. It's correct Vineyard sign, but it is rudimentary compared to the fluency Nancy and I have. I try to sketch a box with windows, then lay down the pencil. "George was the artist; I'm a writer."

"Describe it to me." Nancy's uncle reaches for the paper. His sketch is primitive but adequate. "And there's only the one drive leading to the house?"

I nod, remembering my first, excited approach to the Vale. All I didn't know then.

"Would you be seen from the house or stables if I let you out before reaching the main entrance?" he inquires.

"Certainly," I reply. "The drive isn't framed by a row of trees. There's nowhere to hide."

"You still have the key to Beatrice's cell?" he asks.

"I smuggled it away in my trunk."

I'm half pantomiming to make the discussion simpler for him.

"Do you think Mr. Culper has taken leave?" Nancy asks.

"I hope Ben is still there, but we can't count on it," I sign.

"No," Jeremiah Skiffe signs. "We'll base the plan around the three of us and the staff we're likely to encounter. Culper, did you say? The name is familiar." He rubs his hands together before he describes the actions each of us will take. His derring-do reminds me of his niece.

"Sissy" (it embarrasses me to call her that) packs lunch and extra blankets while Jeremiah Skiffe's driver prepares the horses and carriage. I pat the blankets, peek in the food basket, and sign "thank you." Sissy is not accustomed to being addressed. She daringly meets my eyes and nods.

Our transportation is elegant but not ostentatious. It suits me fine. This is no time for fairy tales. We ride at a regular pace. It's part of the plan to seem natural rather than fevered. A gentleman from Quincy making a lone trip to consider taking up summer residence in Waltham.

Nancy drums a tune on a cushion with her fingers. I can see her mouth making corresponding noises. Her uncle takes a sip from a silver flask and peers out the window. He seems to have all the time in the world. His calm demeanor stills my shivers. We have one chance to rescue Beatrice before we're found out. "When we arrive," Jeremiah Skiffe tells us, "I'll ask questions about the area, the grounds, and the house to keep this Mr. Norwich occupied and distracted."

"Better use an alias!" I warn him with Nancy's help. "There's no doubt he read my correspondences with Nancy and may recognize the name Skiffe."

Jeremiah Skiffe nods.

"We'll sneak away and look for Ben in the greenhouse. The kitchen door was left unlocked when I was there, but I don't know if circumstances have changed; we might need his help getting in, as well as with Beatrice if she's badly deteriorated in the days since I left."

"And then up the servants' staircase to free a ladybird," Nancy concludes.

I nod and pat my cloak pocket with the key.

When I catch sight of the manor house sunk in a vale, I feel my breath catch. I point, and while Jeremiah Skiffe nods calmly, Nancy strains her neck to see.

"Get down," Jeremiah Skiffe signs, handing us the extra blankets. Even amid his long legs, Nancy fits on the floor and I lie belly down on the opposite seat, trying to make myself smaller under the wool covering. It might seem scary that I can't hear my surroundings, but I think deafness gives me a rare stillness. I imagine I'm a stone.

The horses slow down. The carriage shifts as Jeremiah Skiffe climbs out. I feel him tap the roof twice slowly. That's our code. It means Mrs. Collins is greeting him. Three quick taps mean he's been invited into the manor and our driver has been directed to the stables. The driver knows to get off his seat and check the horses before moving on.

I feel Nancy pat my back. Is the coast really clear? I peek out from under the blanket. She's sitting up. "Time to go," she signs. My face must look stricken. She repeats, "Go!" I remember my student and keep my head down as we crawl out the carriage doors that face the drive rather than the house.

"This is like squatting behind the stone wall watching Andrew Noble collect Vineyard dirt and other scientific samples of the deaf," Nancy signs.

That memory snaps me into the urgency of our task. "Follow me," I sign.

I assume Ellie is preparing tea for Jeremiah Skiffe while Mrs. Collins and possibly Mr. Norwich are giving him a tour of the manor. That was the plan. But any of them could peer out a front window and spot us. We must move quickly.

Nancy follows me around the east wing. Ben's crystal palace looks sharp and dangerous rather than enchanted. The door is locked. I knock repeatedly while Nancy goes round peering through the windows.

"I've never seen anything like it," she signs when she rejoins me. "The plants look healthy. Someone's tending to them."

Could Ben be out of service? Not seeing him, I sign, "We've got to do it without him."

We crouch behind the hedgerow where Ben and I once spotted Mr. Norwich talking to an unfamiliar man. It's a good cover. But we'll have to run to the back of the house. "Go," I sign to Nancy.

I'm counting on the back door to the servants' staircase to be open and pray it was not battened down after Ben and I took leave. Lord, I cannot do what I must for the suffering girl without your Grace.

Nancy pushes it open and turns to me, grinning. "Up." I point, knowing that Jeremiah Skiffe will not prove an endless distraction. I'm used to the spiral staircase, but Nancy almost trips twice and I fear the sounds she makes. Finally, we arrive at Beatrice's door.

"They are shutting her in, but mortaring hasn't been completed," Nancy signs. "I think I can pull some of it down with that awl. At least enough so you can slip through."

She hands the bricks to me, but one drops to the floor. We look at each other in horror. Nancy shakes her hand next to her ear. The noise echoed in the stairwell. We continue our work at a more rapid pace. I push myself through the hole Nancy's made, a small space between wall and door, then manage to turn the key in the lock.

The door flies open. The small windows have been boarded. I feel my way in the dark. I don't sense movement. Where is she? Has she been left in here to die?

I sweat as I crawl. Finally, I bump into something. I run my hands over a bony arm. I rub it till I feel some warmth and the fingers twitch. I can feel breath on my hands. Beatrice is alive!

I pull her toward the door. Her eyes open and close, trying to decide if I'm a dream. Nancy helps Beatrice through the hole in the brick wall. Beatrice is weak at first, almost limp, but she fights us still. What must she think of Nancy or what we intend to do with her? Perhaps she is delusional. She whips around in fear, then looks me in the face. I nod, beseeching her with my eyes to trust me. Hers are wide, but she returns the gesture.

On the staircase, Nancy and I press Beatrice between us. A shaft of light from an open door appears underneath us. Please let it be Nora!

The three of us move as quickly as possible, which means noisily. Who's waiting below? Where's Jeremiah Skiffe?

Nancy gestures for me to slow. I almost snap at her that we don't have time for her spying games, but she must hear something because her head cocks. Beatrice watches her with open fascination. Nancy presses herself against the wall and slinks along it, urging me to do the same.

We reach the ground floor. Freedom is so close I nearly run with Beatrice, but Nancy stretches out her arm, once again triggering my impatience. I feel no vibration save the pounding of my frantic heart. I wish I could hear what she does, just for the moment! Beatrice echoes my frustration and slaps at Nancy's arm, which makes her scowl and nearly earns Beatrice a scalding retort.

Nancy carefully molds herself to the doorframe, bending around it to peer through the butler's pantry into the kitchen. She gestures for us to move quickly to the garden.

But just as I reach the door, Mr. Norwich comes through it from outside. Before I can react, he grabs my arm. I release my hold on Beatrice and push her toward Nancy, signing for her to run. The two bolt, Nancy looking back at me as frightened as I have ever seen her.

Mr. Norwich shakes my shoulders while shouting, spittle landing on my face. I struggle to free myself, prying his fingers and trying to bite them, but they bore into my skin so tightly they will leave marks. He pulls me toward the kitchen. Does he mean to trap me, and then go after Beatrice?

There's a moment of strange, sudden stillness as his eyes glaze over. Suddenly, I fall backward and Mr. Norwich collapses vacantly onto his knees and then forward onto my legs. I'm startled till I look up and see Nora holding a small flatiron pan that she has just used to knock Mr. Norwich senseless. She's still wielding it like a medieval knight, a fiery lock of her hair falling against her forehead. I laugh hysterically till she clasps my hands. We both roll the moaning butler off of my pinned legs. I stand with Nora's help. We briefly embrace. "Fly," she signs.

I catch up to Nancy and Beatrice headed the wrong way, and turn us east toward the hothouse. Jeremiah Skiffe is nowhere in sight. I pray that he is waiting for us in the carriage.

Before we reach the hedgerow, I look back and see Mr. Norwich stumbling after us, holding the back of his head. He seems to be shouting. What if Stephen comes running? I've seen him take down Beatrice without breaking a sweat. Could Nancy and I fend him off?

After heavy exertion, my friend slows just as Mr. Norwich catches up. Nancy opens her mouth to scream. Is she calling her uncle? A figure approaches us. From his movements, I can tell it's Ben! We move toward him. I follow Nancy's gaze to Mr. Norwich, whose eyes are fixed on Ben.

We're caught in the middle as they exchange words. Nancy seems to get a second wind just as Ben leaps like a tough old tiger, and the men begin wrestling on the wet lawn. I jerk my head to say "Let's move."

As we come around the left wing, Jeremiah Skiffe waves to us from the carriage, the door ajar. We approach, and he runs toward us and scoops Beatrice in his arms. We all climb into the carriage. Through the window, I see Mrs. Collins standing on the entry porch. Her hand is raised to her mouth in shock. I feel terrible leaving Nora behind. What fate awaits her after conking her master? She seemed resolved in her actions, so I pray the Lord will watch over her and help us see each other again.

Jeremiah Skiffe doesn't give us details of his actions. He's bolstered by a job well done. "We'll all return to Quincy for now," he signs. "She can convalesce till she's well enough, then we'll try to learn if she has family."

My friend is puffing from her heroic performance, but she shoots me a glare. Whether or not Nancy wanted Beatrice under her roof, she's got her.

We all observe Beatrice watching the Vale as her years of torture there recede in the distance. I know from my own experience the difficulty that yet awaits her. It is hard to break the shackles that remain on one's spirit. She doesn't know where we're going—just away! I point to Nancy and her uncle and make the obvious sign for house, drawing walls with a basic roof on top. She watches me and shakes her head, turning back to the window. She breathes on the glass and writes my name in the mist with her finger. Mary. I hand her the straw doll, and she blinks at it, pressing it to her chest for a moment.

Nancy's hands are uncharacteristically still. Is she resentful of sharing me with Beatrice? Or is she recalling her own history of abuse? She opens the lunch basket and puts it on my lap. Beside me, Beatrice holds my hand as she touches and smells the foods before she bites into a turkey leg. Gold wouldn't be a finer offering.

Chapter Twenty-Two

When we arrive at Jeremiah Skiffe's residence, Beatrice collapses much as I did. Jeremiah Skiffe carries her upstairs to the guest room next to mine. She's obviously uncomfortable being handled by a large stranger but lacks the strength to fuss.

I drape her in one of Nancy's nightgowns. She rubs the excess fabric between her fingertips and smells it, pressing the softness of it to her cheek.

Though I've been paid for my services, I still take responsibility for her. I gently wash her hands and face, tucking a stray wisp of hair behind her ear. She screws up her nose, but do I detect a hint of a smile curling at the corner of her mouth?

I settle her in bed, and she uses her legs to kick the blankets away, turning on her side and pulling her legs up against her chest, arms wrapped around her knees. I reach for the covers and pull them up to her chin, tucking her in as Mama used to do for me when I was a child. Her eyes are already drifting closed, and slumber takes her quickly. I sit on the rocking chair till I'm assured all restlessness is gone.

Once Beatrice is soundly asleep, I find Nancy at the fortepiano. "Our adventure was exhilarating," she signs, "but music brings me back to my world."

"You've made an admirable life for yourself," I sign. She side-eyes me to see if I'm criticizing her. I smile gently.

"It's true," she admits. "I'd take anything but my drunken father whipping me and my mother crying but never protecting me."

"Know," I sign.

"Anything but," she repeats.

"Beatrice isn't safe yet," I sign.

"About that," she signs. "I admit I was intoxicated by the thought of one more adventure with you. But this is your fight. And I've been neglecting my music and the bluestocking cause. I don't know what Uncle has planned, but I can't go on."

"Understand," I sign. "I don't think lesser of you for it."

"I hope you never lose your nobility, Mary."

She moves her hands across the keys. I start to

retire, then turn around. "I forgot to ask you about the standoff between Mr. Norwich and Ben. You heard their exchange. I thought I saw a smile cross your face."

"I can't believe I forgot his treachery!" she signs.

"Ben?"

"No, that scoundrel butler. Apparently, he was a traitor in the War. Never exposed, tarred, or feathered. But the gardener knew. He's been tracking him for years. Camped on the grounds after he was dismissed. He's part of an old spy group, the Culper Ring. They were set up in British-occupied New York. Uncle and I should have caught it when you said the name. They're quite legendary."

"I met an actual spy?" I say. "And a traitor!" The news astonishes me. Mr. Norwich's actions were always criminal in my eyes, even if he were a loyal servant hiding the family's secrets. But I never thought I'd meet a true-life turncoat.

"I wish I'd seen the authorities take him away in manacles," she snickers.

I smile. "I hope that pleasure was granted to his long-suffering staff."

"And his confederate who you witnessed pass him

a letter in the garden. Perhaps they were plotting assassination! What of him?"

I wrap one hand around my head as if I'm tying a noose, then close my eyes and stick out my tongue.

We laugh as we did before my brother, George, died and the world turned upside down. Then I retire to bed, knowing my duties are far from over.

I can hold this version of my friend in my heart. Papa taught me not to dwell on the failings of others in order to elevate myself. Nancy will continue to grow at her own pace, even as I push beyond the boundaries of society. Am I fated to become a renegade like Ezra Brewer?

Chapter
Twenty-Three

I wake up to Beatrice's face peering into my room, her gold-flecked eyes wide. When I spy her, she closes the door quickly and retreats. Did she open every door to find me? Or is she simply exploring and testing the limits of this newfound freedom? I smile as I imagine her giving Jeremiah Skiffe quite the fright.

I wash and dress quickly. Downstairs, I find Beatrice trying to open the main entry, the only door in the house I asked Nancy to lock. When I gently put my hand on her shoulder, she whips around. I read relief in her eyes. I shake my head when she sticks her pinkie in the keyhole. Still, she tugs once more on the door handle, then sticks out her bottom lip. She has discovered the limits to her liberty.

Jeremiah Skiffe comes down the stairs in his night-shirt, and Beatrice hides behind me. He slowly raises his hands to show he's no threat. For obvious reasons, she is frightened of powerful men.

"When we returned yesterday, I sent Sissy to ask

around for cast-off clothes in the girl's size. There should be a package in her room."

I gesture for Beatrice to follow me upstairs. She grasps hold of my skirt like the reins of a horse she's steering.

I pour fresh water in her basin. She cleans her arms and face without my urging. She now seems to relish it, even though the water is cold. She lingers with the cloth, dipping and wringing, and sweeping it slowly across her skin.

I pick up the package and start to open it, but she finishes. I point to the gown and stockings and then to her. She hesitates, wrinkles her nose, and makes a sour face. Does she associate such a wardrobe with the Vale? What was her attire on Cape Cod? I remember Ben removing her boots and stockings. Was she a carefree girl who wandered the dunes barefoot as I once did?

I help her dress. Her figure is skeletal, with bruises old and new. I touch her gently. She doesn't flinch. We practically knocked each other out in the deer park. I laugh at the memory. When she looks at me, I raise my splayed hands like antlers on top of my head. She giggles and looks down grinning. Does she feel a genuine attachment to me? Or does she simply hope to use me to flee? That's how I felt about Nora at Dr. Minot's house. I hope Beatrice feels more.

When we enter the dining room, Nancy is already seated. A hearty breakfast is laid out on the sideboard. I take two china plates and hand one to Beatrice. I fill mine and without instruction, she follows my example. I unfold a napkin in my lap. She does the same. I eat with a fork, while Beatrice observes closely. She has not quite mastered the way to hold her utensils. She makes choices whenever given the slightest liberty. If we had started our lessons in a place like this, imagine the progress we might have made.

I worry about the amount of food Beatrice is consuming. I had to slowly regain my appetite when I was delivered home after my ordeal. I lift my glass of water to remind her to drink between mouthfuls of johnny-cakes, eggs, and sausage. "Sissy" enters several times to clean up, but Jeremiah Skiffe asks her to return when Beatrice is done. Beatrice, for her part, seems more interested in the maid than our host; her eyes follow her around the room.

"That certainly was an adventure," Nancy's uncle

opines. I appreciate that he signs as he speaks. "It was enjoyable to create the character of Phineas Horatio Hobbe, with his irritatingly selective nearsightedness." Laughter goes around.

Beatrice must make an unmelodious sound because Jeremiah Skiffe makes a show of sticking his fingers in his ears. I grit my teeth. Papa and I have discussed this ugly habit of the hearing. Do we deaf cover our eyes if we find someone unpleasing to look at? That would certainly be discourteous. Are manners made for certain people rather than others?

After finishing, Beatrice tries all the doors in the house again. She's suddenly frantic as a rat in a cage, her mind fixated on escaping. I need to demonstrate that communication is the key she needs most. I want to see how much she can write.

After trailing her through the house several more times, I guide her to the dining table, where I lay out paper, pen, and ink, and seat her across from me. I write our names on the paper, pointing to each of us. Then I write: *Where did you come from?*

She runs a finger over the letters as I flood with anticipation. My expectations lift as I watch her.

Could she give me the clue that I'm looking for? Instead, she crumples the paper and throws it on the floor.

Determined, I draw a rudimentary house. I point to her, then to it. She becomes agitated but doesn't leave. I continue with the drawing. It's my house in Chilmark. I draw Mama and Papa and Sam and Yellow Leg. I primitively fill in the trees and the fence and draw two lines for the high road, walking my pointer and middle finger along it.

She stops my hand and moves her mouth. I cover my ears and shake my head. I reach up to cover her ears, which causes her to reel back and bump into the sideboard. Her eyes widen. She opens and closes her hands, not exactly making signs but not defensively either. Has she realized we're alike? It's a startling revelation for a maltreated deaf person in the hearing world to come across another.

I urge her back to the table and draw another simple house. When I write *Beatrice* inside, she tries to take the paper, but I hold it down with my wrists. I draw another house next door. I'm challenging her.

She slides her chair and again hits the sideboard,

bringing Jeremiah Skiffe into the room. I sign for him to stay back as I begin to write my name again, *M-A.* She pulls the pen from my hand and spills the bottle of ink.

I almost correct her when she starts to make a shape other than *R*, but instinct tells me to let her be. It looks like an *S.* Jeremiah Skiffe quietly comes closer as Beatrice finishes her word. *MASHPEE.*

I turn to my host. "Mashpee! That's on Cape Cod! Mashpee is one of the larger Wampanoag communities left."

He looks shaken, even tearful. "It certainly is."

Beatrice turns to the paper again. Her attempt to write more words is fruitless. The alphabet, neatly done, is incomprehensible. I've seen the Greek alphabet in George's books, but not this. What could it be?

Pointing to the house I drew with her name on it, she starts to expand the landscape. She has an artful hand for her age. She draws small houses in a group on the other side of the page. Shaded trees and a prominent building on a hill. Four figures. Three of different heights wear pants like men. The last figure has wild hair with black circles for facial features and wears a loose shirt or dress. Is this her mother, the one taken to an asylum? The likeness is far different from her portrait.

As we stand stunned, Beatrice scoops all the papers and throws them into the fireplace. She crouches to watch them burn. She rocks on her feet, a grieving expression on her face.

"You said there was some kind of scandal in the family," Jeremiah Skiffe signs. "What if bringing her there is a grave mistake?"

"Do you have another plan?" I sign. "Could she possibly become more unmoored?"

"You're not old enough to realize—"

I cut him off. "I'm in charge of her well-being. Would you prefer that she continues to deteriorate in mind and body? Because that's what will happen. I don't know her history, but she's carrying the weight of it even as she tries to keep it hidden. The chance of something is better than nothing."

Nancy, who has entered the room, looks back and forth between us. She's uncommonly still.

Jeremiah Skiffe's hands stammer. "The drawing may be a rough sort of map. Or simply a child's drawing.

I'll make inquiries. The Vale is well known, and people do like gossip."

When he exits the room, I collapse on the floor next to Beatrice. She pats my head gently. I look up at her, wiping my nose along the back of my arm. She purses her mouth sympathetically and strokes my hair.

My girl, I'm bringing you back. I hope it's what you want.

Not knowing what we'll find in Mashpee or how long we'll be there, Jeremiah Skiffe has my trunk shipped back to the Vineyard. I send along a letter to Mama and Papa telling them that I'm no longer in service at the Vale. I say I'm traveling with Jeremiah Skiffe to the Cape, omitting all other details.

As we prepare to depart, "Sissy" tweaks Beatrice's nose playfully, which makes her laugh. I hope "Sissy" resembles someone doting where we're going. I nod my head in thanks; she returns the gesture.

I don't know when I'll see Nancy again. We embrace and take each other in. Was it so long ago we were running up and down the beach in drenched shifts and sandy legs, dreaming what then seemed unimaginable? I sign, "I'll miss you! Let me know when you have your first recital in Boston. Oh, and tell Molly it was most felicitous to meet her."

Before mounting the carriage, I turn back to my friend. "The cause of women's liberation will be stronger if it includes all women. Ask 'Sissy' her proper name and invite her to your next meeting." I give her a challenging wink.

Nancy sighs and rolls her eyes, but I don't take it as an outright rejection. It's in her nature to be a mule.

As Beatrice climbs into the carriage, she slides to the floor on her knees and stomach before planting herself on the seat. I shake my head at her playful insolence. We're side by side in more ways than one.

Nancy and I wave our arms wildly at each other through the carriage window and throw kisses as I pull away. Beatrice amusingly joins in.

The cart's rhythm is soothing. We ride toward Boston and then east to the Cape. Jeremiah Skiffe isn't engaging company like Ezra Brewer at his most provocative. His signing has improved in my presence. But I can't expect stories about runaway carriages with phantom drivers. Perhaps due to a full stomach,

Beatrice is less alert and falls into a deep slumber. I watch the scenery—small patches of snow, bare trees with their arms raised like dancers—while questions line up in my mind. I must ask them carefully, as my host has revealed his prejudices.

I know some about Mashpee people from what Papa told me. Following their defeat in King Philip's War in 1676, Wampanoag people were organized into either Indian Districts or praying towns, if they had become Christians. These areas were on or near all the old original village sites, so people still lived where they always had. The government of Massachusetts Bay in Boston designated Mashpee as one of four reservations in Massachusetts, and ordered people from other Wampanoag communities to move to Mashpee, Aquinnah, or Herring Pond. Sometimes people were allowed to govern themselves, but other times they had a white overseer supposedly there to help them with their own affairs. Like the Wampanoag on the Vineyard, it's a history of colonial oppression and greed.

"Did anyone in Quincy know anything of Beatrice or her mother?" I ask.

"I took a stroll and made some strategic visits to

neighbors' homes. The Vale is a much-admired estate in these parts," he signs. "Very progressive in the innovations you describe, like the hothouse. The family is well thought of, but there's talk in elite circles. And among disgruntled former servants. I did not mention the girl or her condition, as I had no desire to slander them without a full accounting of the events that led up to your arrival."

"Slander?" I sign. "You've seen her condition."

"Let's remember the staff was tasked with her care."

It's useless to quarrel, but I'm put on edge. I take a deep breath and remember the dictum of patience.

"Had anyone heard of the woman who married a farmer on Cape Cod?" I ask.

"That's most delicate," Jeremiah Skiffe replies. "But one talkative housemaid entertained me in the absence of her mistress. She worked at the Vale briefly before your friend arrived. It's a fact that the family's eldest daughter turned her back on society and married poorly. She was always thought to be unstable and rejected her family's attempts to put her right."

What might Molly make of this story? The wayward young lady who was forced to conform and disobeyed. Can we ever be honest rather than bowing to decorum?

"And did they mention a child?" I sign.

"Not at all," he signs. "I've been thinking on that. Since the girl was at the Vale, there's certainly a family connection no matter how scandalous."

"I agree."

"That writing of Mashpee and the feral state the girl is in," he signs animatedly, "combined with the mark of strangulation on her neck. Well, I can't help but wonder if there was a savage attack on her parents and the girl was taken as an Indian captive."

My face must show disgust. "The Wampanoag," I inform him, "are not known for killing settlers nor kidnapping children."

"That's the official version, Mary," he signs. "You must realize that these things happen wherever we are compelled to live close together."

"Who is compelled to live with whom?" I ask. "We invaded their land."

I'm brushed aside. What is it with these Skiffes?

Take one brother out of the country and dress him up in the city, but he still promotes false and hateful notions. I stare out the window to avoid further discourse. His primary communication is oral speech, so he will be Beatrice's spokesperson on Cape Cod. How can I stand up for my charge? I will need to be fearless like Sally.

Chapter Twenty-Four

My stomach is upset, and not just from the long ride or nerves. The trip has already been soured by Jeremiah Skiffe. I wish Nancy had decided to come along. As the roads become more rural, the carriage jolts and rattles. Beatrice remains sound asleep. When the driver stops for a flock of sheep who stubbornly lie in our path, my host gets out to help shoo them away. I take the opportunity to shake Beatrice awake. I cannot do it. I feel her chest; her breathing is steady and deep. I smell my breath and then hers on the palm of my hand. It's slightly metallic.

Jeremiah Skiffe climbs back into the carriage, and we start to drive slowly, mindful of the sheep that are near.

When he looks up and smiles at me, I ask, "What physic did you put in our breakfast?"

"Excuse me?" he signs unconvincingly.

"This is the most I've seen Beatrice sleep since we met. She's normally inquisitive and creative. My stomach is upset. I'm only slightly drowsy, but I ate far less. I expect you to tell me the truth."

"Oh," he signs, "I instructed Sissy to introduce a mild sedative into the eggs. I didn't have time to pull you aside and let you know. But I noticed you ate little as the girl gorged."

"You did that without my permission," I sign. "I don't find it acceptable, and I don't think my parents would either."

"I would tell your parents it was an error that you ingested it," he signs. "I'm sure they would understand about the girl if I described her state."

"Her name is Beatrice," I sign. "And don't be so certain what my parents would believe."

"You are . . ." He reaches for the sign but cannot remember it, so finger-spells "impetuous."

"I think my mind is clear," I reply.

"You're guilty of kidnapping," he signs, "which my niece and I aided and abetted."

"Why are you doing this, then?" I ask. "To be rid of us or out of guilt for my brother's death? Maybe both."

"That's cruel, Mary," he signs. "I'm risking my reputation by involving myself in this affair. I'm escorting you and Beatrice to the Cape. I will do my best to find the truth for you there."

I bite my tongue. The sooner we get there the better. I'll have to study the writings of Mary Wollstonecraft. What does she say about men who claim to support the cause, then take charge?

I start to smell dry, salty sea air all around us. It makes me long for home. If it weren't for helping Beatrice, I would forget the whole adventure. What have I learned from it? That people can be terrible in all sorts of manner, that they cow the decent and meek. Wealth and position do not denote character. I observed that in family and friends. For some reason, it takes going away to completely fathom it.

I see private homes and factories, even ships moored in a harbor. The driver stops again and opens the door for Jeremiah Skiffe.

"Please wait here," he implores. "It's better if I make inquiries with the people of Barnstable. Mashpee is close by, but we need more information before we approach. You and Beatrice can certainly disembark when we arrive, and I'm certain it's safe for ladyfolk. She is starting to stir. Attend to her needs and your own."

233

I nod. When he walks away, I take Beatrice's hands and gently rub them between mine. Her eyes open and close as she comes to consciousness. Her cheeks puff up, and I open the carriage door just in time for her to vomit in the sand. I wish I had fresh water to rinse both our mouths. I use the sleeve of my cloak to wipe her lips. She begins to look around, take deep breaths, and reach her hands out the window. Four senses are as perceptive as five, especially when stimulated. Are memories trickling into her mind?

While I detest Mr. Skiffe's methods, I'm glad that Beatrice is too drowsy to leap from the carriage never to be seen again. It seems like forever waiting for him to return.

Finally, he climbs into the carriage after talking to the driver. We don't start moving.

"Did you find anyone with information about Beatrice and her family?" I ask.

"Indeed, I did." He nods. "It's not a pretty story. I don't know how much you should be exposed to."

"Please tell me," I sign. "I apologize if I was ill-mannered, even insolent."

"Accepted." He nods. "It's a complicated matter. Her mother married a man, a poor farmer, named Brown from Sandwich, a town in this county. We've already passed through it. She was troubled and the marriage dissolved, though not legally, mind you. They never had children. Then she became acquainted with a man from this place and . . ."

"They had a child."

"Yes," he says. "It's not like you haven't heard of similar cases on the Vineyard."

"Then what happened?" I ask anxiously. Beatrice is growing fidgety beside me.

"Her mother became hysterical," he describes sadly. "She returned alone to her husband, Brown, but it was no good. The father couldn't care for the child on his own. He is a gentleman, but his father is Mashpee and gave her to his sister and her family to raise. Nothing else is known."

"The three men in Beatrice's drawing? I cannot believe the Wampanoag harmed the child," I sign. "Why would they? Especially if she's family. There are missing pieces of this puzzle."

"Perhaps you are right," he signs. "But be prepared

235

for the worst. I will take you and the girl, I mean Beatrice, there because I cannot see what else to do with her. But you must follow my lead. Promise me that, Mary."

What can I say? I nod, knowing I'll go back on my word, if necessary, for Beatrice's well-being.

To focus my mind, I make mental notes.

1. Beatrice's mother was born at the Vale and chose to marry Mr. Brown, a poor farmer from Sandwich, Cape Cod.
2. She had a tryst with an unnamed man from Barnstable Village.
3. Beatrice's mother was allegedly touched in mind and left her child with the girl's father before returning to Mr. Brown.
4. The unnamed man was unable to care for the deaf child. He gave her to the only person who'd take her in, his father, Beatrice's grandfather, a Mashpee man.

"I wonder which house she drew on the map she made," I sign. "Her father's house here in Barnstable?"

"An interesting question," he concedes. "If there's truth to it."

We continue on as the sun begins to set. When you're on a shoreline, the streaks of color and light permeate everything. I point out the window for Beatrice. I'm pleased with her delighted response. She's reawakening. A child I'm not acquainted with but would like to know.

"The roads are poor on the Indian land," Jeremiah Skiffe signs. "We can only ride so far and then we'll have to walk. I have a firearm."

This isn't what I imagined, and I dread Jeremiah Skiffe doing something hasty. But the only way through is forward.

Jeremiah Skiffe has the idea to tie Beatrice's wrist to his own with a rope. I understand his concern, but blanch. I suggest that she and I be tethered. He reluctantly agrees. Beatrice is less amenable when I present her with the hemp twine. Her gaunt face goes pale, and when I take her hand, she struggles. I wave my hands exaggeratedly to get her attention and show her that I'm tying one end to my own wrist. Her nostrils flare from her heavy breaths, and I wonder with a pounding heart if this is a step too far.

Pursing her mouth to show her displeasure, she hands me her arm. She can't help an involuntary jerk as I tie the rope around her slender wrist. I am weighted with guilt for restraining her again, but I try to make it a game by swinging our tied arms.

We see houses gathered together, smaller than the ones in Barnstable. I think again of Beatrice's map, how she drew the cluster of houses apart from the one with her name. Was she indicating the distance between Barnstable and Mashpee?

As we walk toward the dwellings, Beatrice starts tugging at the rope between us. She halts and tries to pull me back in the direction of the carriage. Jeremiah Skiffe notices and pushes us forward. Beatrice digs in her heels. She opens her mouth and raises her free hand to her throat. I feel her terror, and suddenly regret all of my choices. Everything in me wants to let her break free, but I cannot.

Just then, a tall Wampanoag woman comes out of one of the houses. Her tan face is wrinkled and friendly, and her gray hair is tied in a bun. She carries a bucket, probably to fetch well water. When she sees us, she freezes in her tracks. I can't imagine what we look like to anyone who doesn't know our purpose. A man and two girls, obviously not from these parts, tied with a rope. Jeremiah Skiffe raises his hand to speak. Before he has a chance, I start laughing at his sureness in all matters. He looks vexed till the woman laughs too.

Jeremiah Skiffe is relieved to learn she speaks English and politely interprets her question, "How can I help you?"

He replies, "I'm looking for the younger girl's grandfather."

She asks, "Who told you he was here?"

"A man in Barnstable," he speaks and signs. "It's a long story."

She leans forward, studying impoverished Beatrice, who meets her gaze. The woman shakes her head in uncertainty. Could this be someone from Beatrice's early life? She reaches to tweak her nose like "Sissy" did. Beatrice cautiously steps out of reach and the woman drops her hand.

"I have to finish preparing food," the woman says, a bit distracted. "But we're having a meeting soon. You're welcome to join us."

"Thank you. Where will it be?"

I see Beatrice's drawing and imagine the building on the hill before I look to see where the woman is pointing.

"We'll wait there," Jeremiah Skiffe says as the woman goes about her business.

We climb to the building. It is white with two doors and two windows at the front. The sides have two windows with black shutters. It looks like a plainer version of the church and Meeting House in Chilmark. Jeremiah Skiffe tries the door and finds it open. As soon as we enter, Beatrice collapses in a fit.

Chapter Twenty-Five

I've never seen Beatrice like this, not even at the Vale. It's not just a child kicking and screaming. She seems to be having a seizure.

"What was in that physic?" I demand.

"It couldn't have done this," Jeremiah Skiffe insists. The panic in his eyes gives me pause.

"Help untie me before she breaks her arm or mine!"

He unfastens the rope, but she still writhes on the wooden floor. I kneel beside her but cannot get close enough to try to soothe her.

"What will they say when they come?" Jeremiah Skiffe asks. I take his concern as self-interest.

"They'll ask who she is and what we've done to her," I reply. "How do you intend to respond?"

"The girl is hysterical like her mother," he signs.

"That will not do," I sign. "The signs of abuse and starvation are upon her."

The doors open, and at least twenty-five men and women file in. I'm distressed, but not intimidated. If

Jeremiah Skiffe is unwise enough to brandish his firearm, any number of situations could occur.

A Wampanoag man steps forward and speaks. Jeremiah Skiffe holds his hat in his hands and does not interpret for me. The woman we met approaches Beatrice. She bends down and takes her face in her hands. Calmed, Beatrice sits up and wipes away her fog of tears. The woman's mouth moves, but she does not sign. Is she speaking Wôpanâak? Does Beatrice respond? How is that possible for a deaf girl? I've never seen their language written. It may explain the unrecognizable alphabet that Beatrice wrote at Jeremiah Skiffe's dining table. Why didn't that occur to me?

The chairs are placed in a circle, and Jeremiah Skiffe gestures for me to sit.

"What are you telling them?" I demand. "Would you please interpret? I'm very much involved in Beatrice's situation. She's my charge."

"Mary," he signs without speaking, "it's best if I handle this."

It's hard to resist kicking him. I can't imagine he's handling it well. The mood is becoming increasingly chilly. Has he accused them of garroting Beatrice yet?

How can I get the Mashpee people to listen to me? I decide to say my piece the only way I can. I hope someone intuits my meaning.

I follow Mrs. Pye's daring actions in her classroom by standing on a chair. I certainly have a rapt audience as I perform in Vineyard sign the events that occurred from the time I received Nora's initial letter in Chilmark till I arrived in this Meeting House. I try to put as much clarity and passion into my facial expression and body language as I do in my signs.

At one point, Jeremiah Skiffe takes my right hand. Whether he means to still my speech or pull me down to the floor, I know not. I shake him off. The audience looks to Beatrice, who regards me with sincerity. Five men and two women, including the one who welcomed us to the village, turn their backs and talk among themselves.

"Now listen here," Jeremiah Skiffe speaks and signs. No one pays any mind to his attempt to reassert dominance. I see him reach for his pocket and jump off the chair.

"Don't you dare pull out your firearm," I warn, downplaying the obvious sign for "gun."

"They are conspiring against us," he signs with a mixture of irritation and fear.

"Wait a moment," I urge. I think, *This is how it happens. Innocent Wampanoag men and women are shot in the back while we claim self-defense and are absolved.*

Fortunately, they turn back toward us, and a man raises his hands and speaks slowly.

"What did he say?"

Jeremiah Skiffe, who's still on high guard, signs, "They're fetching someone they believe can help us. Mary, perhaps it's best if you run."

"I will do no such thing," I sign. "We're in a church in a Christianized town, and nobody has been anything but courteous. I will stay with Beatrice. You can leave if you choose. Your obligation is fulfilled."

I admit I'm stunned when he pulls out his gun and holds it at his hip as he backs out of the Meeting House. A man swiftly exits behind him. Through a front window, I watch the man follow him. Jeremiah Skiffe raises the pistol, and my heart stops. I believe he shoots into the air because the man behind him does not drop to the ground. Still, others run out to check on him. Jeremiah Skiffe appears to be running toward his carriage. No one follows him. They didn't ask for trouble; we brought it.

I move toward Beatrice and kneel with my arms around her. I remain calm but smile nervously, realizing I am now abandoned with no communication or passage home. Seconds pass like hours. Beatrice pats my hands. Her gaze remains watchful, but she is more tranquil than I have ever seen her. The woman with whom she was speaking stands by us.

The door opens, and the men return. Indeed, they fetched someone who can help. It's Sally's father, my old friend Thomas Richards!

I can't imagine anyone I'd prefer to see at such a moment. His smooth black face has not aged. But gray dusts his short-cropped hair, and his hands show signs of frostbite and hard labor. He is a shrewd man, as well as a bridge between white deaf and Wampanoag communities. He smiles to find me in this of all places.

"Good to see you, Mary," he signs with ease. "Who's the friend you have brought with you?" I tell him, and then his eyes slowly look over Beatrice, taking in every bruise and the gauntness that makes her look older than her eight years. Sometimes I forget that I'm not even twice her age. She should return to childhood games and fun. I know it won't be easy. Her years weren't simply lost but stolen. She's seen and experienced things no girl should have.

I release Beatrice and jump up to hug Thomas. I feel tears choke my throat.

"Hush," he soothes. "We'll get this sorted out."

I tell him of my journey and all I know of Beatrice's history. He occasionally shakes his head. He does not question my veracity. He explains to the others. I read recognition on some of their faces. The woman we met begins to cry. She reaches for Beatrice, who folds warmly into her arms. Beatrice moves her mouth, and the woman nods as if she understands completely.

I'm incredulous. "How did she learn oral speech?"

Thomas interprets for me. "No one knew sign language when Beatrice was brought here as a baby. She doesn't completely lack hearing as you do. She could understand her auntie speaking by touching her throat and watching her lips. How clever she was! She began to repeat the sounds, in her own way. Her auntie and grandfather understood."

"I've been told that she makes odd clicking sounds. Is that part of the language?"

"No," he replies. "That's a result of her . . . injury. But she's still understood, as if you lost a hand but still signed. May it never be so."

Beatrice turns to me before she's led out of the Meeting House. I walk forward and draw the little straw doll from my pocket, pressing it into her palm. She looks at it for a long moment, and I think I see her blink away misty tears. She looks up at me. "Girl," she repeats the sign I taught her. My knees almost buckle. She presses the doll to her chest and leaves.

I almost follow, but Thomas holds me back. "You must let her go. She'll begin to heal. As a bud frozen in an early frost, if carefully nurtured, can bloom brightly as any other." He gently cups his large hands, then opens them to show the necessity of letting go.

"Is her grandfather here?" I ask.

"He's passed on," he signs. "But the woman you first encountered is her auntie and the others love her dearly. Thank you for bringing her home."

"What exactly happened, Thomas? I don't mean

to intrude, but she was my responsibility and—"

"You did well for her," he signs. "After I find you passage back to the Vineyard, I'll tell you what I learned. But I need to know if Jeremiah Skiffe or his niece will tell any settlers that she has been returned to Mashpee. That could bring danger."

"Mr. Skiffe feels we kidnapped her," I sign. "For the sake of his social standing and business interests, I'm sure he will wash his hands of the whole affair and instruct Nancy to do the same."

"I'm glad to see you say it," he signs. "He is correct about her being kidnapped."

As the group starts to exit the Meeting House, a young, smiling man only a couple of inches taller than I gestures for me to follow. Thomas nods his approval before leaving for the wharf to find a boat that will steer me home.

We enter the largest home in the village. I'm offered a place to wash up and a round bread, bumpy and savory, to fill my gurgling stomach. I've made an arc from Chilmark to the Vale and Quincy, and now this welcoming abode. It's taught me you can genuinely find light amid the darkness. I offer to help clean up after the meal. Without awkwardness or embarrassment, residents point and pantomime to communicate. I smile in appreciation. What is next for me?

I manage to communicate that I wish to see Beatrice one more time. Her auntie brings her to bid me farewell. She wears a blue skirt and a blouse borrowed from her little cousin, simple leather shoes, and a wool shawl about her shoulders. Her cut hair makes short braids. I'm amazed by her transformation. Beatrice's face lights up when she sees me. I've never seen her with such a big smile, as she comes up and takes my hand. She is taking me into her confidence, on her terms.

She puts her hands over her ears and mouth, to indicate my particular deafness. I nod. She repeats more signs I made at the Vale. She is the teacher now. Will she invent a sign language with some Vineyard sign to help her communicate? What a thrilling notion! I look around for someone to help us communicate. But Beatrice is whisked away to rest, I imagine.

Perhaps I wasn't a complete failure in my first teaching position. Looking back, my mistakes weren't all disasters. I hope I have another chance to try. I have a little money of my own. Maybe I will travel elsewhere one day.

Thomas returns and says my ship will leave in an hour. "I'll wait on the wharf with you," he signs. I'm glad for his company and fascinated to uncover the gaps in Beatrice's past, like the woman she drew with black circles instead of a mouth and eyes. But first things first.

"How did you find yourself here?" I ask. "Sally told me you signed on to another whaling expedition. I'm sorry about the loss of your wife. Everything I knew about Helen was strong and good."

He stares out at the dark water.

"I'm here visiting kin. My first wife in slavery was sold away from me," he signs. "I said I'd never give my heart so completely again. But I couldn't turn away from a lady so captivating as Helen. Illness and disease are brutal discriminators."

His fists are clenched. I almost reach out to touch his hand, but it's not my place to take away his anger.

I look at him and think about his history. Sally helped me understand how different her family is, not just from settlers but from Wampanoag without African roots. Does Thomas receive inferior treatment from his whaling crews? The thought disturbs me.

"Sally misses you," I sign. "She wants you back."

"My daughter is very independent," he signs.

I look into his eyes and smile. "She still needs her papa."

"There's a young man in Aquinnah," he signs.

I grin. "She didn't mention it."

"I don't want her to see me grieving," he signs. "I'm just an elder, set in my ways, who will hold her back."

"I know that's not true," I sign. "And, you see, I told her I owed her a favor."

He laughs. "What did you get into this time?"

"Don't you mind about that," I sign slyly. "But you could clear my accounts if you came back with me. Just stop for a bit."

"The whaler I signed on to sprung a leak. I was let off my contract," he admits. "I thought I'd stay around here and do some odd jobs."

"Like reunite poor deaf girls with their families," I sign. "What did happen to Beatrice?"

"I'm sure there are many versions of the story," he

signs. "But the one that I've been told and believe is that her mother gave birth to a deaf child out of wedlock. She thought it was a curse for going against her family. She returned to her husband without the baby. At a loss to raise a daughter, Beatrice's birth father gave her to his father, whose sister and family raised her. Her mother came, allegedly to visit. Beatrice was playing near the Meeting House, when her own mother tried to kill her by tying a cord around her neck. Beatrice's cousin, another healer like my Sally, discovered them in time and saved the girl."

"No wonder Beatrice pitched a fit when we entered the building," I sign. "How could a mother do that to her only child?"

"You know deafness is misunderstood, and considered an affliction. Perhaps she felt guilty. Maybe there was a sickness in her soul. In any case, it sounds like she's also paid a heavy price."

"You said Beatrice was kidnapped," I remember.

"They immediately dispatched a carriage to bring her back to the Vale," he signs. "The whole Mashpee community wanted the mother charged for attempting to kill her own daughter. However, given her retrieval by her family, and that Beatrice had survived, although traumatized, the overseer of their Indian District would not heed their pleas to have justice done for the little girl. They also knew the child would likely be taken away if the whole story came out, which was inevitable."

"That's not fair!" I sign.

"No, it isn't," he replies. "The colonial system empowers English families to take Indian children into indentured servitude. Think about the number of times you have seen a Wampanoag child living in this situation. Wampanoag people really have no way to prevent it from happening. In this case, I think the mother's family couldn't stand the idea of a relative, even one they despised, being raised as a 'squaw.' A hateful word the settlers use against our women."

"So under pretense of taking Beatrice into household indenture, they shut her away as a prisoner at the Vale?" I sign incredulously. "And the mother locked in an asylum."

"The attainment of a purity that's never existed poisons the people and land we share," he signs.

"I've experienced my share of that," I sign. "I

imagine it's much harder for you, Sally, and Beatrice's family."

"While we all contend with it, there are varying degrees," he signs. "Until the men who have appointed themselves landowners and leaders have a change of heart, we are all in danger."

We are quiet for a few moments. How can I best fight this spreading poison?

"Well," I sign. "Here's my boat. You've told the captain about my deafness and where I'm going, correct?"

"I did," he signs. "But I'm thinking I'd better come along just to make sure. And to check on my own gal too."

Even exhaustion can't keep me from breaking into a grin. The sky is a dark velvet cloak without the brightness of moon or stars. But we're homeward bound!

Chapter Twenty-Six

There's no landing party waiting for us. It will be a big surprise for Mama and Papa, as my trunk and note will arrive later. Thomas thanks the captain, and we trek up to the high road and walk up-island. Some of the houses we pass have lights that guide our way. The Hillmans' home, which always seemed impressive, looks quaint. Wait till I tell Sarah about meeting John Adams!

Thomas pulls me to the side of the road. He must hear a cart coming. It slows down before we arrive at the edge of my farm. It's Mr. and Mrs. Pye. They have a lantern to see ahead, but they're incredulous when it shines on my face.

"Mary," Mrs. Pye signs, "that can't possibly be you. How did you get here so fast? Your mother told me she posted the letter yesterday."

I shake my head to show I don't understand. "I just traveled from Cape Cod on a boat with Mr. Richards," I sign.

"Thomas," Mr. Pye says, swinging the lantern, "is that you?"

"Yes, sir," he signs. "It seems like we may have unwittingly entered a situation."

A situation? Mama wrote a letter calling me home? What's going on?

Mr. Pye grabs my hand and pulls me up onto the seat between him and his wife.

"Do you want to ride in the cart as far as Reverend Lee's?" Mr. Pye asks Thomas.

"Thank you, but I think I'll walk back to Aquinnah," he signs. "I have a speech to prepare."

"You could stop at the farm to see Eamon," I sign. "But beware of the ginger rascals!"

"Maybe another time." He smiles and walks on in the darkness. I wish I could witness his reunion with Sally.

"We'd better get going," Mrs. Pye signs under the lantern. "There isn't any time to waste."

"Is Reverend Lee ill?" I ask. This is a very strange homecoming. "Perhaps I should see Mama and Papa first."

"They'll be there," Mr. Pye assures me. "And Reverend Lee is right as rain."

256

He and Mrs. Pye exchange a glance and off we go. The time must be past midnight. Why are they on the road? Why are Mama and Papa at Reverend Lee's? The air is frostier than I noticed on the boat, where we hovered near the stove. It's so dark I feel we're driving through a cave.

When we pull up to the vicarage, there are other carts parked outside. If I didn't know better, I'd think I never woke up after collapsing at the Skiffe house in Quincy. But this is stranger and more vivid than a dream.

We enter the vicarage, which is well lit, and I can finally see everyone. Mr. or Mrs. Pye must announce my arrival because Mama turns and rushes over to me.

"Mary, can it really be you?" she asks, looking me up and down.

"Everyone keeps asking that!" I sign. "It's a very long story, but I arrived on a boat from Cape Cod with Thomas Richards tonight."

"Are you just stopping?" she signs one-handed, holding my other hand tight.

"I'm no longer in service at the Vale," I tell her and

257

Papa, who comes up behind me and folds me into a warm embrace.

Reverend Lee's housekeeper, the Widow Tilton, offers me a plate of food. I politely decline.

"Can someone tell me why there's a party at the vicarage on a bitter winter night?"

"Not party," Papa signs. "You come home just in time."

"What wrong?" I ask.

"Ezra Brewer." Papa uses his name sign, the two-handed letter *E* rolling forward like waves.

"Mama mentioned in her letter that he's not feeling well," I sign. "Is he here, at the vicarage?"

I see Papa sigh. Mama signs, "He tried to stay in that ramshackle house of his on the beach, wouldn't let a doctor attend to him. Claimed he ate a bad oyster or caught a chill from the north wind."

"What's wrong with him?" I ask.

"We think he had a heart attack, but he wouldn't keep still," Papa continues as Mama wipes her eyes. "He kept going on about needing to check the lobster traps and how the *Dog* wanted repairs and there wasn't anyone else who could do it right. He was on the cutter, hammering and sawing, when he finally collapsed."

"I knew something was wrong when I saw his black cat in the high road," Mr. Pye interjects. "Just sitting there cleaning herself. When I stopped, she dashed down to the boat. Her master couldn't stand on his own, so I laid him in the back of my cart and brought him here."

"He hasn't been the most agreeable houseguest with Reverend Lee," Mrs. Pye signs, "and the Widow Tilton has threatened to quit more than twice."

"He's been asking for you, Mary," Papa signs quietly. "He knew you'd come back. Said he owed you an apology no less."

"Pshaw," I sign as Ezra Brewer might. "We had a minor quarrel as he was set on spooking me when I left."

"Let me see if he's up to a visit from you," Papa signs and walks away.

"Can it wait till tomorrow morning?" I ask Mama. "I'm starting to realize how tired I am. I long for a good night's sleep in my own bed."

"Mary," she signs. "By sunrise, he's likely to be gone."

"Back to his cottage on the beach?" I ask. "That's just like him, not to want all this fuss around him."

"No, dear," she signs. "He's getting ready to pass on."

I stumble backward till Mr. Pye steadies me. "You must be wrong," I tell her. "He always says he'll live to be one hundred and two, so he has some way to go."

Reverend Lee joins us. "It's the Lord who chooses the time, and it's nigh."

I search the sad faces watching me. I'm looking for someone to laugh and tell me it's all a joke.

Papa returns. "He ready for you."

Mama walks me to the guest room door. "I go with you?"

"No," I sign. "Just two of us best."

Closing the door behind me, I recognize the room as the one Andrew Noble briefly occupied, where I secretly searched his belongings. There are flowers and candles covering all the surfaces. I'm not the only one who finds it distasteful.

"Mary." He raises his gnarled hands, full of eight times ten years of stories and spite. The most expressive signer I've ever known. "Welcome to my funeral."

"Stop it," I sign, nearing the bed.

"What else would you call it?" he signs. "The opposite of a christening, but still with the prayers. I despise cut flowers and scented candles. It's the old biddies' way of getting back at me."

"Why did you want to see me?" I ask. "Don't tell me you're going to apologize."

"I wanted to know how it went, this engagement of yours on the mainland."

"You must be joking," I sign, tickling my nose.

"Do I look like it?"

"It was awful, worse than I could have imagined," I admit. "The girl was literally chained up in her own filth. The butler not only looked down his nose at our kind, but he was also a traitor to the nation."

"Nice company you've been keeping. Where's the girl?"

"She's home, with family."

"Aye, I knew you'd succeed."

"You didn't sound like it," I sign.

"Don't mind my mockery and bile," he signs. "I thought you knew better. You were always my horse in the race."

"I never mind you much," I sign, tearing up. "What race are you talking about?"

"The only one that counts," he signs.

He stretches his hands as far as he can, searching the blanket next to him. Smithy surprises me by leaping from a nearby chair. She curls up at his hip.

"I hereby bequeath your father my favorite wicker chair," he signs. "Whichever seaman grabs my tackle and lobster traps first has a right to it. I can't imagine anyone will want to live in my ramshackle palace. You may go there anytime; it's a good spot for a thinker who doesn't follow the town's proprieties. And the *Dog*: scrub the decks, raise the sails, lay us out in the bunk, lift the anchor, and cast it away . . ."

"You can't die," I insist.

"Just watch me," he signs with a jerk of his head. He begins to sign some more words and then he's too still. I run for the door and Mama. She calls the men into the room. I stand to the side as they try to revive him, to no avail.

Does anyone else notice his one open eye focused on me till Reverend Lee closes it with a benediction?

Everyone wants to know what we said. I keep most of it private. When it's discovered Smithy went with him, I leave the room.

I sit on the burgundy sofa in the parlor. Everyone else rushes around, except Mrs. Pye, who sits next to me.

"I'm sorry for the loss of your friend," she signs. "You've had enough grief. But we can't control these things."

I nod slowly, trying to comprehend.

"Your pupil?" she inquires.

"Beatrice," I sign. "I thought she needed me, but after letting her go, I don't know who I'll be without her."

"Exactly," she signs. "But there will be another and another. Some you'll remember forever." She gently pinches my cheek. "Never stop looking ahead."

I think in most cases Mrs. Pye's second principle must prove true. *Where you come from is less important than what you achieve.* In Beatrice's case, her belonging in the Mashpee tribe, the only people who accepted her wholly, is tied to any future achievements. The same will always be true for me and the Vineyard.

Someday I'll share these observations with my mentor.

I walk outside. The sky is pitch, a mourning shroud over the village.

Back home, I sleep and wake and eat and sleep. A tedious routine that brings no relief.

Six days later, on my way home from one of my walks, I can no longer see the *Dog* on the horizon. My hands fly with thoughts and feelings.

Ezra Brewer's last words were "in excelsis." People believe he didn't have a chance to finish with "Deo." The assumed "Gloria in excelsis Deo" serves as a saving grace to many villagers, proof of his innate goodness in the end. I imagine him shaking a stubborn fist. He was never churchgoing folk. And I feel the message was directed at me. "In excelsis" literally translates to "in the highest degree." What if he meant in all things? To be battered by the sea but not yield, to fight invisible enemies and not let down your guard.

I've thought I was meant to be many things. Dutiful daughter, devoted sister, writer of tales. I will finish the history of the deaf on our island community. But is writing enough without courageous action?

Must I be constrained by Mama's expectations? Or society's prejudices? I will always be imperfect to many. Why try to appease them?

I helped a girl who was like me but a lot less lucky. The difference between victims and survivors is whether you're found in time. We cannot swim while the other sinks. I imagine the lonely and wild out there bobbing on the waves. Waiting to be washed ashore or dragged out by the tide. Names unknown, dreams forgotten.

The shackles that cowed me are broken. My girlish games are put away. This island will no longer hold me.

HEREDITARY DEAFNESS ON MARTHA'S VINEYARD

From 1640 through the late 1800s, hereditary deafness was common on Martha's Vineyard, especially in the town of Chilmark. Deafness was a recessive trait that affected white settlers equally. The genetic mutation produced complete deafness at birth with no associated anomalies. The population had a unique form of sign language, Martha's Vineyard Sign Language (MVSL), which was spoken by Deaf and hearing residents. MVSL aided the creation of a national sign language—American Sign Language (ASL). The last native MVSL speaker, Katie West, died in 1952.

THE WAMPANOAG NATION

There are two federally recognized tribes in Massachusetts: the Wampanoag Tribe of Gay Head (Aquinnah) on Noepe or Martha's Vineyard, and the Mashpee Wampanoag Tribe on Cape Cod. The Wampanoag Nation also includes other tribes: the Chappaquiddick Wampanoag Tribe of Chappaquiddick Island, and the Herring Pond Wampanoag Tribe of south Plymouth.

The Wampanoag Nation, also known as the People of the First Light, have lived in present-day eastern Massachusetts and eastern Rhode Island for more than twelve thousand years. In

2007, the Mashpee Wampanoag received status as a federally recognized sovereign tribe. In 2015, the federal government announced that 150 acres in Mashpee and 170 acres in Taunton would be recognized as the Tribe's reservation land. As of this writing, there are roughly 2,600 enrolled citizens in the Mashpee Wampanoag Tribe.

On March 27, 2020, under the Trump administration and during the COVID-19 pandemic, the Tribal Council was informed by the federal Bureau of Indian Affairs that reservation designation would be rescinded and, with the consent of the US Department of the Interior, over three hundred acres of land would be removed from the federal trust. The hashtag #IStandWithMashpee and peaceful protests spread. On June 6, 2020, a US District Court overturned the Department of Interior's ruling, instructing them to reassess their claim and in the meantime preserve the reservation status of the tribe's designated reservation land. The DOI appealed the decision. In February 2021, the Biden administration's Interior Department withdrew the appeal, securing tribal sovereignty.

⌁ INDIAN CHILD WELFARE ACT (ICWA)

Since First Contact, Indigenous children across the US have been forcibly removed from their homes and often not reunited with their families and tribes, whether due to slavery, indentured servitude, assimilation in cruel boarding schools, or other purposes. The Indian Child Welfare Act of 1978 is a federal law that governs jurisdiction over the removal of Native American children from their families in custody, foster care, and adoption cases. ICWA was created in response to the excessively high number of Indian children who were separated from their homes, families, and American Indian cultures as a whole. Before the enactment of ICWA, as many as 25 to 35 percent of all Indian children were involuntarily placed in mainly non-Indian homes that had no relation to American Indian cultures after being removed from mostly intact American Indian families with extended family networks. This law is currently under attack in several US states.

⌐ "LADYBIRD, LADYBIRD"

There are several versions of this traditional rhyme, which has been dated to at least 1774. I chose the one listed on the Poetry Foundation website: https://www.poetryfoundation.org/. There you can find more rhymes attributed to Mother Goose and a brief history of who she may have been.

⟶ THE VALE

The Lyman Estate (sometimes called the Vale) is a historic manor in Waltham, Massachusetts. It was the Lyman family's summer residence for over 150 years. Designed by Salem architect Samuel McIntire and completed in 1798, the Federal-style mansion consisted originally of the home, lawns, gardens, woodlands, and a deer park. Formal gatherings were held in the grand ballroom, with its high ceiling, large windows, and marble fireplace. The greenhouse (or hothouse) was constructed in the late 1700s and is believed to be the oldest in the United States. I became enchanted by the house when I visited years ago. So did filmmaker Greta Gerwig, who used it as Mrs. Gardner's house in her 2019 adaptation of Louisa May Alcott's *Little Women*. Today the house is much changed, but you can still spot the original ballroom in the film. None of the events in my novel that take place at the estate are based on fact or the Lyman family.

⟶ MARY WOLLSTONECRAFT

Mary Wollstonecraft (1759–1797) was an English writer, early white feminist philosopher, and champion for women's causes. Her best known book, *A Vindication of the Rights of Woman*

(1792), argues that men are not intrinsically superior to women, but only appear so because women lack the same levels of education. She died less than two weeks after giving birth to her second daughter, Mary Shelley, who would go on to write the classic story *Frankenstein*.

⁓ANNE SULLIVAN AND HELEN KELLER

Anne Sullivan (1866–1936) is well-known as the teacher of Helen Keller (1880–1968), a Deafblind child. When she was just twenty, Sullivan, with great wisdom and resourcefulness, taught Keller to communicate, bringing both women much acclaim. Sullivan's letters written between 1886 and 1933, related to the education of Keller and often sent to Michael Anagnos, the director of the Perkins School for the Blind, influenced the way I drew Mary's interactions with Beatrice. As Mrs. Pye reminds Mary, Sullivan practiced caution but also threw it to the wind. She wasn't set in a rigorous curriculum—she used all objects at hand as teaching tools, and she realized when it was time to remove Keller from her stifling, albeit familiar environment. She also suffered physical attack from the young Keller—who raged at not being able to communicate with the world—but still she persisted. It's important to note that Sullivan's letters reflect her racism against the Kellers' servants, including Black children.

⟶ THE MONSTER OF GLAMIS

Thomas Lyon-Bowes was born on October 21, 1821 to Thomas Lyon-Bowes (Lord Glamis) and Charlotte Lyon-Bowes. Robert Douglas's Peerage of Scotland recorded that Thomas was "born and died" on the same day. And yet decades later, rumors began to spread that the disfigured child had actually been brought up in isolation, concealed in a secret chamber in Glamis Castle, Scotland—which was closed off after his death. This story gave rise to the legend of the "Monster of Glamis." There is factual basis that the chamber exists. The absence of a tombstone for the child is seen to support the story.

When I read this story in my youth, it made a great impression on me as a drastic example of unwanted disabled children.

⌒ ACKNOWLEDGMENTS

This book happened more quickly than *Show Me a Sign*. And in times of trouble, I'm ever more grateful for my partners and friends.

To my incomparable Scholastic team. My editor Tracy Mack, we've come a long way since you first took a chance on me as a writer! Thank you for honoring my way of being, respecting my instincts, improving my weaknesses, and pulling it all together in ways that startle me. Your artistry and care shine through these pages. Associate Editor Benjamin Gartenberg, I appreciate that you had more input into shaping this story and your immediate replies to all questions and deft communication with authenticity readers. Marijka Kostiw, your expert book design makes the written words look better. My publicist, Elisabeth Ferrari, for always sending me good news when I need it most and being willing to navigate my accommodations during a most unusual year. Thanks to the essential work of Erin Berger, Lizette Serrano, Emily Heddleson, Rachel Feld, Julia Eisler, Jody Stigliano, Elizabeth Whiting, Jacqueline Rubin, Dan Moser, and Nikki Mutch. Nikki, we'll always have NEIBA 2019, which you made magical.

I wasn't sure I'd ever find meaningful representation. This book wouldn't exist without the hard work and support of my agent, Leslie Zampetti of Dunham Literary, Inc. You've been with me through good times and bad, after hours and weekend chats, with full appreciation and understanding of my unique needs. You're loyal, fierce, and funny. We made it—and there's more to come! Thanks to Jennie Dunham too.

Bobbie Bensur, it was a joy to meet you when you did a B & T Title Talk Book Buzz at my library. Thanks for being an early enthusiast.

Julie Morstad, thank you for creating daring, exceptional jacket art, which literally shows another side of Mary and conveys the relationship at the heart of the story and the need for communication between all Deaf and Hard of Hearing (DHH) children and their caregivers. Thank you Penny Gamble-Williams, activist and Spiritual Leader of the Chappaquiddick Tribe of the Wampanoag Nation, for consenting to do another authenticity read. Your words are always carefully chosen and your perceptions astute. I worked hard to meet the challenge you assigned me. Thanks to Linda Coombs, Aquinnah Wampanoag, Wampanoag historian and independent scholar, for your thorough and specific input on the text. Thanks to Andrea Shettle for your suggestions and feedback on DHH representation. The Longbow-McHenry family continues to enrich my understanding of Afro-Indigenous identity and history. Thanks to Kamil for sharing your experience as a below-knee amputee. And young Liz for telling me about your cleft lip—I made Ellie a dancer like you.

To all the critics, bloggers, and fellow children's book

authors who embraced and promoted *Show Me a Sign*. Too numerous to name, but I'd be remiss without mentioning Betsy Bird, Alex Gino, Louisa Hufstader, Mike Jung, Erin Entrada Kelly, Cicely Lewis, Sheena McFeely, Angie Manfredi, Meg Medina, Lyn Miller-Lachmann, Kimiko Pettis, Debbie Reese, Ali Schlipp, Lisa Yee, Christina Soontornvat, Ann E. Burg, Aida Salazar, Mr. Schu, Indigo's Bookshelf, and We Need Diverse Books!

And to steadfast friends Edith Campbell, Alia Jones, Debbie Lewis, Gabi Sheremet, and Ross Woodbridge. My extraordinarily brilliant sister Jean is the best counsel, resource, and believer in my life.

To all the DHH kids and teens of 2020 who were moved behind the protections of digital screens and masks. Who didn't receive services mandated by their IEPs, were given online assignments without interpreters or captions, and were the only ASL-fluent members in their families. To those who "fell behind": I tried to stop the gaps. Then I wrote this for you. Because you matter—always—to someone.

The text of this book was set in 12 point Adobe Garamond Pro, a contemporary typeface family based on the roman types of Claude Garamond and the italic types of Robert Granjon.

The title type and author name were hand-lettered by Julie Morstad.

The jacket art was created with pencil and digitally rendered by Julie Morstad.

The book was printed at LSC Communications.

Production was overseen by Melissa Schirmer.

Manufacturing was supervised by Irene Chan.

The book was designed by Marijka Kostiw and edited by Tracy Mack.